NUNC STANS

A FERRY TALE

A Novella and Stories

PJ PICCIRILLO

D1598982

CATAMOUNT
PRESS

an imprint of Sunbury Press, Inc.
Mechanicsburg, PA USA

an imprint of Sunbury Press, Inc.
Mechanicsburg, PA USA

For information about special discounts for bulk purchases, please contact Sunbury Press Orders Dept. at (855) 338-8359 or orders@sunburypress.com.

To request one of our authors for speaking engagements or book signings, please contact Sunbury Press Publicity Dept. at publicity@sunburypress.com.

FIRST CATAMOUNT PRESS EDITION: January 2022

Set in Adobe Garamond Pro | Interior design by Crystal Devine | Cover design by Tyler Handa | Edited by Abigail Henson | Author photos by David A. Woodring.

Publisher's Cataloging-in-Publication Data
Names: Piccirillo, PJ, author.
Title: Nunc Stans—a ferry tale: a novella and stories / PJ Piccirillo.
Description: First trade paperback edition. | Mechanicsburg, PA : Catamount Press, 2022.
Summary: From the title story's beautiful reflection on a couple's grief, guilt, and awakenings in the aftermath of a stillbirth, to a graduate student discovering in the trauma of an assault the prerogative of her own fertility and identity, conflicted hearts long for human connection while whispers from vivid landscapes beg that these troubled characters turn their searches inward.
Identifiers: ISBN : 978-1-62006-872-4 (softcover).
Subjects: FICTION / General | FICTION / Short Stories (single author) | FICTION / Small Town & Rural.

Product of the United States of America
0 1 1 2 3 5 8 13 21 34 55

Continue the Enlightenment!

For our sons

JP, Michelangelo, and Antonio

Who teach me all the good things

. . . for those who love, time is not.
—Henry Van Dyke

CONTENTS

NUNC STANS—A FERRY TALE

The wind. There to buffet the flag or not, skulked about the nooks of his mind. Fickle, more of a factor in navigation than was the urge of the current as it pushed at cross purposes to Randolf's route, constant but bumpy beneath the black sky-mirror of the river top, beneath the flat bottom of the ferry.

Breezes may have coursed the valley out of the North back when the wedding-goers and horse and buggy boarded from the landing at dusk, but something had been astir in the western distance across the river, echoes of electricity blinking in a smoky cloud swell cresting Berry Mountain. Not enough, though, to light an evening pass were another ferry departing that far shore.

Not that, he'd thought. Leave it alone.

And now, with night fallen and the ferry under way, there came white lashes of lightning. At least they gave him peeks at the horse, tense already, as was the most eager of the Amish to make this final run, the blond-bearded fellow, Ezra.

Ezra the reader—always a library book on his lap, going back to his boyhood when he crossed with his parents. A reader as was Randolf, except Ezra grew to prefer heavy literary tomes and philosophical works. Kant, Randolf recalled, a name he knew from a high school history teacher who'd waxed lyrical about great philosophers.

From the edge of the wooden deck, Ezra watched ahead, glanced back confounded—a nervous Noah in the foretaste of the storm.

These were the last of the Amish Randolf would ferry back to their side; he'd been at it since midafternoon. In front of the cabin, under the little porch roof, the rest of them huddled on benches, the storm flashing pictures: women with white aprons flapping about their dress skirts, some skirts navy, others black, the tails of their dark veils wagging in the wind; men in charcoal coats and snow-white shirts holding down their round-brimmed hats. Disappearing then to pipe embers.

With every flicker, Randolf's eyes snapped between the horse and the palest of those seated, Ezra's Becca, a broad-hipped woman with spectacles shaped like the palms of soup spoons, a girl really—one very near to giving a little sibling to the twin toddlers practically gnawing at her flanks.

The chief concern with the wind wasn't in navigating the caprice of its moods and meanders. That was a routine obstacle to steering the river ferry—a barn-red, wooden affair, really just a paddle-wheeled houseboat affixed to an 80-foot deck of planking, the flat as it was called, and that, little more than a severed single-lane bridge 14 inches off the water. Even though the ferry was keel-less, even though in drawing only twelve inches of water, its superstructure took a breeze as a sail took a typhoon, the real worry was what a sudden change in the wind foretold. A ferryman had to predict the descent of fog or blinding snow, the coming of the damned lightning. So he learned to decipher the wind's taste, feel the cant of it off the mountains and against the cabin, read its flow, sweep or stutter, the shapes of its ripples on the water. In fifty years ferrying, he'd cataloged into his mind the prophesy of every peculiarity, right down to the fife or hiss of a gust sliced by the hogging cables. Though capricious and indifferent, the wind was a thing to rely upon.

But his alertness had dulled. Unless he summoned his senses anymore, the wind stealthed right past him. From the time he'd loaded the first trip until dusk, he'd been heedless of that north breeze, prevailing, he now realized, only to try to catch a fool unawares. When the last passengers boarded, it had about-faced, slung-shot upriver, and even then, he hadn't considered what that meant; instead, he powered the prow toward a storm any fool knew held a bead on them. Then the breeze gathered into huffs, chuting in invisible antithesis to the current, forces squeezing at the age-stiffened maneuvers and reactions he invoked against the perils of night ferrying. He should have at least smelled the direct hit of this storm in the air, done what it was too late to do now: abandon this crossing.

He could feel, back behind the droning engine and plunging paddles, the east shore dissolve like a river shoal in a February freshet. Hand over hand, he spun the wheel to the starboard, hard into his upriver arc. Out beyond the hats and bonnets and horse and buggy that he could no longer see, the storm clouds had blanked any illumination of the night sky in the cradle of the mountains, that beacon by which he held his course. The steel of river chill twisted into his hands. Their aches, as many and varied as the bones, had crippled him to a fair-weather fer-ryman—back before he'd given it up altogether. He stretched his fingers, reached forward, and swung open the cabin's window-pane, watched for the flag in the next lightning flare. No need. The ferry tilted as a mid-gust turn of the wind came around and caught him straight in his face. He throttled all the fuel the old flathead Ford could cackle through her cylinders.

Now the thunder—boom and clatter fast on the tails of the electric veins fragmenting the clouds above Berry Mountain. In the next flash, blonde Ezra appeared at the window frame.

"It's the horse," he hollered—rare animation from an Amish. The flag snapped twice. Then strange calm, that pause of gather-ing breath.

Randolf squeezed the top spoke of the wheel, ready to swing to port. "I'll try to go back."

Ezra's wordlessness told him he was shaking his head no.

She would not turn, the storm in its fury beautiful, disgraced if seen as an inconvenience to navigation.

&

The first time she saw him, he was on leave from the Navy, still a gangly boy, so quiet he might have been shell-shocked— had he been to Korea. Bernice was a town girl; he from over there among chicken farms and corn canes on the broader, fertile side of the valley, the son of a river miner who was the son of a timber raftsman. Each had known the river in a different way, she a painter of it, he a river rat who'd grown up plying the water on handmade rafts, a wooden canoe that day they met.

She wasn't much of a talker herself, unless it came to painting. And who wanted to hear of that? So the meeting had been mostly polite grins and embarrassed glances. He'd poled his way along the ferry weir while she sat on a bench above the high, weedy bank, her easel to her side where it wouldn't sully her view. Before spotting him out there, she'd watched the horizon over Berry Mountain until the light of the sun rising behind her blushed the first puffs of western clouds into pink roses. Then the color caught in tendrils of mist ghosting along the far half of the river. As he emerged from these, the water at his feet, the mountain on his shoulder, she knew she'd put him there, this hatless and songless gondolier defying that insistent charge to the Chesapeake. She would paint perfect empowerment—the geese to the darkness, the otter to the depths.

But only in her mind then. She left him out, stored in her heart the dry seed of the image.

&

So long as electricity flashed into the tar bucket of blackness, he had the occasional shape of Berry Mountain to help unfuddle his feel for the current against the steering oar as the wind jabbed variously at the cabin walls. And now the rain—with the lurching of the storm, it alternately thrashed and prattled across the ferry's flat roof.

The lightning took flickering fits, drumrolls of thunder announcing each deluge. Between these, he could hear the twins' muffled yawling and the older Amish chattering at their benches to soothe the pregnant mother, themselves.

Ezra appeared again, the brim of his black hat breaching the cabin light, water dripping onto Randolf's hand atop the wheel. "Why we headed so hard upriver?"

Randolf ignored him. With only that oar to steer this keelless craft, he was taking every precaution. He'd plod farther up the river than usual and use the leeway to concentrate on the wheel after he turned the bow for the landing, not having to fiddle at the same time with the throttle to fight the current. Besides, he needed the extra margin in case the wind settled into the course of the river. And tried to push them into the weir.

Ezra insisted. "We got to get acrosst. Outta this." The hat brim swiveled, turned back. "The horse."

The rain upon the tarpaper roof came in an even crackle now. Soon the wind, steadying itself, would settle in where it chose. Just not southerly, Randolf thought. "I have to make a long sweep," he said. "The wind."

The hat brim disappeared, returned a moment later. "That horse is trying to chew a post. We get another pass of lightning, and it'll be his feet, not his mouth, full of nerves."

"Then unhitch." Randolf peered to the port, hoping for a glimpse of Berry Mountain. He turned the wheel to the starboard, compensating for a slow turn of the wind. "She gets tangled up hauling that buggy off the deck, we're in trouble." He added in his mind: *trouble in the middle of a rising river.* "Think of your kids."

Ezra extended his head closer, his blond hair in the glow of the cabin light bronzed at his temples. He squinted, eyes flitting back and forth as if he scanned a poster notice on the pilot's face. "I *am* thinking of my kids when I think of that horse."

~

She'd just dabbed a gauzy blush at the upper margin of the mist grazing the eastern half of the river. Down before her, he glided his poling canoe to the riverbank, the hull rasping against stones and mussel shells, hissing across sand. The canoe stopped, his feet keeping the landward momentum, a fluid movement, like those war boats depositing cargo. While he'd come across as smoothly as a bell's peel, a grace seemed to leave the scene after that release.

Then he was out of sight at the foot of the bank, and her vision for the painting, even though she had finished the composition in her mind, lost its soul. It was the most profound, edifying event she'd have in art. Without him, the power of the arrangement she'd conceived and that had moved through her was gone. She rummaged the paint lessons she remembered, searching for a way to regain what she'd felt. But exercises of the mind could no more summon inspiration than hold the sunlight streaming through the mist. She'd have to wait and hope.

He reappeared, dragging his canoe up the bank, clear of the shifty waterline. His military crop sheened in the morning light like the dollop of ivory black on the palette she'd set on the bench. With the nail of her index finger, she traced on her skirt the boxy contour of his head with its sharply edged jaw, chin, and temple. His lips and brow, fixed in a kind of head start to a smile, were not so exact—an exceptional detail to a common shape, such as attracted her painter's eye.

He walked within feet of her before nodding. When he kept going, the knot that had cinched around her heart at the loss of the painting's composition pulled tight again. His close presence, Bernice realized, had loosened it with a wisp of what she'd lost. "You must have left in the dark," she said, at once scolding the impetuosity of her otherwise silent curiosity.

Stopping, he turned and watched the river as an egret landed on a water-sculpted bulb of rock downstream of the ferry channel. She saw in his stare—shameless in this pause before acknowledging her—that he was trained in studying such things, helpless against it maybe. As she waited, the profundity of the elusive composition swept through her. She could have wept, except she was too good of a painter by then.

Finally, he rocked his head up and down. He looked across the grassy riverfront to the street, and Bernice couldn't help wondering if he searched for someone waiting in a car. He wore khaki pants, loose except at sturdy thighs, and in the way of the old tug pilots, he'd tied a blue handkerchief at his throat.

But he remained beside her, occasionally turning an eye to her painting, as a man thought he stole peeps at the V of a woman's blouse; in fact, his every attention to the painting aroused the muddling of excitement and violation churned by those glances. Which she admitted afterward—with forced gratefulness—he never gave her.

She would learn in days to follow he'd come across to visit the river-mining company about a pension promised to his father, ailing, gasping with weakened lungs. And then to inquire on helping with the ferry during his leave—what with no work on the coal diggers lately, even part-time.

He took his last glance at the painting, then squinted off toward the risen sun. "It's not just your eyes you cross it by," he said.

Wishing she could pick up her pencil and tablet and capture that gaze, sweeps now horizontal and oblique, Bernice waited for more. Then she realized he'd come back to her comment about having started off in the dark. "Nor paint it," she said.

At that, he mulled the river. She could tell his way was to size things. He traced the course as though reading a ticker tape, measured the distance between shores, the weight of the air licking the surface. He contained the scene within magnitudes and math—a way she couldn't comprehend but thought she needed to.

"Most people," she said, "don't understand that. About painting from more than the eyes."

Finally, the smile. "We have a secret then."

⁓

Handsome and precise though his brass instruments were, he rarely navigated by them. The compass couldn't see a sandbar, and consulting it would delay his calculations and reactions by a second, which in the worst conditions could mean the inches between a successful landing and a twirling flight down a fickle river. A quarter of the way into this run, the rain dousing from the distance any shore lights by which to place himself, he might have benefitted from having checked his bearings a few times, particularly given such a fast rise and rush of the river. He thought about these. This storm didn't account for them; other deluges on the tributaries did, likely sending into the swifter drift floating hazards—trees.

He arced wider to push his mid-river apex even farther upstream. But this sudden force of the river lamed the thrust of a fully laden ferry—something he should have heeded at boarding, not out here where his wits, lame themselves, told him too late that in altering his course he'd confused that homing sense he'd now need to find his way to the landing.

Could have and should have—the coda of his life.

He squeezed the wheel, closed his eyes, and shook his head to reset the workings of his brain. He'd learned the value of thinking in extremes, had shaken up foul-weather runs by throttling up and to hell with correcting by degrees with some middling scheme. He concentrated. Though it took longer than it used to, too long maybe, an idea came. He'd aim right now at his best guess for the landing, and bull full-power with the bow edged obliquely into the current. He'd land straight on, not turn and drift in backward like usual. But he was as likely to misjudge his shot and get caught on the weir—if it weren't too deeply submerged. That was all the worse, for then they'd be hurled into faster water and be hung up on a rock, the deck likely washing under, how far downriver nobody knew.

Willing his arms into motion, Randolf steered as fast as he could toward shore. With the sudden sideways glide, the women let out a mass, gulping gasp—eerie ode to the wind howling through the porch stanchions. Harness leather creaked in time to the horse's nerves as she blew and stomped, Ezra coming and steadying himself with a hand on the sill. "What did that mean?"

Randolf watched past Ezra, lest he miss a burst of lightning by which to check his dead reckoning. He might have conjured what he wanted, for there appeared a jittering picture-show of mountains against a gloom-gray sky. So askew was the prospect from what he'd expected, it dizzied him—the long spine of Berry Mountain was nearly starboard. He spun back the wheel. And as though he could spirit away an ember of that electricity, he strained for a shore light to aim for.

Or one out there.

Delicately, careful not to arouse the memories he'd buried, Randolf reached into the back of his mind for maneuvers he'd known for fighting the current, the effort muddled in the mental exercise of blanking the ache of cramping hands. He dared to wish for her intuition; there'd likely be no thinking a way out of here, his reasoning hindered not just by concentrating on more than one thing, but the suffocating blackness, infinite and profound as the nothingness he'd conceded that last night he'd ferried.

In the next spate of lightning, the horse yanked the buggy forward, reared onto her back legs, and came down with her fore-hooves skating the lip of the fallboard. She tripped onto one knee, the foot of the other leg splashing into the water, and the twins wailed out to that indifferent abyss.

∾

She decided the impressions of the river on her eye and in her heart better served her stowed, that she could call upon them at home another day. From the distance of a different time and place, her work felt less reportage and more discovery—minutiae of light and perspective that seemed unremarkable on-scene whispered into her strokes. They proved distinguishing; she'd been too prosy, hadn't given way to impulses. Still, a painter of the river needed to be near it every day, close to its purl and the source of that cool, fusty respiration that had surrounded her all her life, as distilled there as the fume in a boat's bilge.

He worked as the ferryman the second week of his leave, waving to her on the bank upon landing. Yes, she'd hoped he'd get the work—for her painting, of course, to have him out there again that she might glimpse what had passed through her as he'd crossed out of the fog.

So she sat on the bench the mornings of that week with her incomplete painting on her easel—except the day it poured— furious, down-pelting paroxysms lashing stripes across the river. Even that day, from under the hood of her slicker, she studied that scene, the wet rubber of her upturned collar lapels cupping the tang of the churned riverbed, the Susquehanna valley at its most temperamental.

All week she watched his crossings and watched between his crossings, the river as ferry route and not, but always the river, him occupying it, and it him, whether he was out there or not.

~

The following May, she found out he'd come back for good. He'd shown up in her father's dry goods and hardware store on the square, pointed above the shelves, and asked whether the girl whose paintings hung there still went to the river.

"What else did he say?" Bernice asked when her father remembered to mention it a week later. Her immediate reaction was relief that her painting of a man poling across the river, in which there was still no man poling across the river, was not for sale with the others above the ladder track. It remained in her room unfinished, its barely beating heart waiting for her to fathom what had moved through her as he'd come out of the fog. Maybe with time, she kept thinking.

Her father shrugged, engrossed in the ledger he reckoned on the counter. "Just that he knew you from the landing. He's starting to work on the ferry." He glanced out the window where his name arced backward in black letters. "Ferry pilot," he said, and chuckled. "Lot of sense in that when there's a bridge coming through. But what do you expect from a Navy boy? River rat, no less."

She went to the door and turned the knob. "There will be no bridge," she said. Stepping out, she thought of the folly of townspeople, the irony. "Ridiculous," she whispered, then looked over her shoulder at her river paintings.

~

The next morning, Bernice went to the white wooden door hinged to a post along the shoreline at the landing. She swung it to face the water, signaling to the ferryman where he checked with binoculars on the other side. She climbed the bank to the bench and waited for the little red shuttle to churn across the river.

Except for its lazy wake, the silent, sluggish ferry at a distance and with no cars on its deck appeared more an abandoned raft, the cabin and paddlewheel some odd cargo. As it neared, she saw there were no riders. Randolf turned the craft upriver and cut the power to drift the stern into the landing, probably wondering what sort of child pranked a crossing so early in the day. But when he trotted onto the deck to tie off, he sneaked a glance her way; he'd already spotted her. He pretended to look about for his passengers, finally feigning surprise at seeing her. "Did you hail the ferry?" he shouted.

Bernice stuffed her hands into the pockets of her cardigan and looked up the valley. She rose to her feet and started through the dewy grass to the gravel launch road. When she turned his way, he let down the fallboard ramp and waited.

Standing before the ferry, she nodded out at the morning haze, which down here held what seemed a heavy, collective decay of the river's creatures. "If you teach me to pole off and snub, I'll help you." Watching the wet toe of her blue tennis shoe scuff gravel, she realized why she spoke in such a deep voice—she'd anticipated the doubt and embarrassment that had turned his eyes away. "I need to be on the river," she said, looking up. "Show me."

Bare desire, he could buy. Randolf grinned and waved her onto the deck.

≈

She came every day. And before long, the paradox presented itself: though meanings in the river's nuances reached her more clearly on the ferry, she had to all but forsake her art, painting only on a rare evening. She'd volunteered with hopes of intimacy with the place, yet it dammed in her breast instead of flowed out the camel hairs of her brushes.

∾

He told himself that being out of practice, he just wasn't limber, his reflexes so dull tonight. He'd always faced a faster current as thoughtlessly as he'd wade a swimming hole, something dependable, typically slow to change, and even when not, the change itself dependably predictable. Now he faltered along as if sorting complications. The sluggishness made him see how he'd once been shaped to the job, the mallard holding to the current. Maybe the harsh price of knowing a quality was losing it.

The lightning brightened only the clouds now. He heard Ezra and an elderly Amish out at the edge of the fallboard coax the mare to her feet. Then Ezra came and asked that the flood-lamp be turned on to calm her. Randolf had intended to leave it off until he probed for the landing—it would obscure reference lights that might appear on the shore, and besides, given his reaction time, it'd be too late to steer away from any floating tree the feeble beam picked out. Yet there was cause to turn it on for a moment; swells in the water could give bearings to prove his latest dead-reckoning, which put him mid-river. He switched the floodlight. Slow eddies told him he was in deeper water, much too close to the weir and losing headway. He cut the wheel starboard fast as he could. The sway upon the sudden illumination of water sent the black mare to blowing and prancing and Ezra out to the fallboard where he seized her in a neck hold, a posture at complete odds with a soothing phrase he hummed into her ear, "*Nunc stans. Nunc stans . . .*"

"What's that?" Randolf said, something in it trying to calm his own fear, the vague disquiet he'd carried in his craw for so long. Ezra ignored him.

Hard as Randolf tried to align the bow into the current that he might gain on it, the river plowed the ferry to one side or the other. Off the port, he spotted the channel breaking over the weir, the water beyond boiling across un-dredged shallows.

"Hold on," he hollered. Though he straightened the ferry, the wheel jerked as the steering oar caught the rocks of the weir, and the river sucked them sideways, Randolf's equilibrium swooping away, leaving him papery and queasy. The port side of the hull slammed the weir, and he motored down as the flat bottom ground across the stones and the sternwheel scud-scud-scudded upon them, the bawling frame members accompanying the horse's whinny and the shrieks of the children.

∾

Finally jaded by an indifferent river, he hadn't ferried for five years. But Warren Stewart, the retired machinist who now owned the business, came to him, asking that he help out the Amish. Randolf had grown up among them—good neighbors— and had hauled them to visit town markets, doctors, and banks for forty-five years. Stewart explained that Randolf would spend the morning shuttling families from the groom's community on the west side of the river; one of theirs was marrying a girl from the farmland beyond town. After the wedding, Randolf would return them. Ten trips at most, a few with buggies.

Though Stewart said they trusted him with their horses more than they trusted young pilots, Randolf sensed he asked as much to lift him out of tedium.

∾

Nobody bought her paintings. It was one thing to look at them in her father's store, to think of the quaintness of a river scene in the dining room, but another to pay for it. And everyone had ideas on how those "pictures" could be truer to life.

None of that mattered to Bernice on the river, away from her father's complaints that if painting couldn't earn her a living, she should stock shelves and refill bins. Or marry. She began to wonder herself if they weren't mere river pictures, snapshots of an accident of ice and tectonics, photographs that taxed the hand, her eye just a distorted lens.

The steady strength and purl of the river were sculpting her mind, the smell of it fuel in her lungs. It was another world on the water, indifferent to people's business and opinions—this from her, now a commercial carrier.

With fair weather and an ideal channel depth, the journey took fifteen minutes, a routine wading of the current for the pilot. Never fully fixed on the ferry's course, he seemed comfortable in some unconscious relationship with the Susquehanna, free to talk to Bernice, to watch diving gulls. The river, though a presence real and incessant, was underlying for him, like dinner music.

Because Randolf made the first run from the opposite shore, her workday—if you could call it a workday when you weren't getting paid—began when he landed at dawn on the town side. She would jump aboard, tie off the ferry, and let down the fallboard for a ramp.

Bernice's busy time was at departure and landing, the most likely points in journeys for boats and planes to perish, Randolf had told her. During the between time on the river, a beautifully empty pause that seemed a thing infinite, she stood at the lip of the fallboard skating over the sky-reflection, away from chatty passengers.

One May morning, on their first return to the town side, she caught him watching her. She'd leaned against the grill of an almond-brown Studebaker to take in the sun crowning a mountain beyond town. Its beams kindled the smoldering mist with the same eerie yellow that emitted from the stacks of the steam engines the miners fed on their coal-digger rafts. Bernice glanced over her shoulder. A sunrise head-on was nice enough, but celebrity, kitschy even—she preferred the quieter echoes of light beneath the heavens the sun was off to occupy. Instead, she met his eyes in the shadowed cabin.

They did not look away as had been their still-bashful tendency, an awkwardness she believed reflected how either of them were of a wrong sort to work together, each bringing a different sensibility to this ferry business. Randolf, for instance, viewed navigating difficult conditions as a matter of precise calculations. At the same time, she believed a ferryman did not master a tricky current, instead figured out how to obey it. The pilot gave himself enough margin of error against the river to get away with a controlled crash. To Randolf, the surly Susquehanna was adversary, to her, goddess.

But this frank stare said he'd arrived at ease with his surprise river companion. It embraced Bernice as snugly as did the amphibian air, calm that morning even mid-river.

Though she'd grown up seeing this water separate humans almost as much as it did shores, Bernice wondered how many other paths had merged as people waded fords or paddled canoes of birch bark or pulled cables. How many had beheld the river from its banks in the company of strangers or, for that matter, in art galleries? Individuals were more entwined on these flowing rifts between nations, castes, and languages than at home among neighbors.

She studied the level lines of his brow and chin, spontaneously tracing them on her corduroy trousers. She couldn't help a daughterly affection. *I've got me a River Daddy*, she thought with savory submissiveness. Slipping her hands into her pockets, she drew up her shoulders and turned back to the eastern shore, filled now with a pioneering self-confidence in this work.

୭

In their rural stretch of valley, economic throes passed in sluggish undulations well after and away from impact. Boom meant not an event, rather what people called the offshore stone piers left of the literal "log booms"—stones cribbed eighty years ago by sawmill operators who'd chained strings of timbers between them to corral logs. Most folks didn't mind missing the surges of prosperity; this was in every sense a middle ground of middle people content with constancy.

So the increase in passengers to the point automobiles backed up at the landings must have caught Annie Schultz by surprise. The widow who owned the business responded with uncharacteristic urgency.

During a morning approach in June, Bernice spotted Annie stepping out of her Buick along the riverfront, a large woman given to loose, formless dresses of fabrics as thick and somber as drapes in the old lumber baron mansions beyond her. By the time Bernice tied off, Annie had made it only halfway down the launch road. She waited for the exiting cars to pass, staring out from her broad, flat face, which appeared dumb and bewildered—deceptively so, for generations of townspeople knew a schoolteacher's intelligence and motherly sympathies pooled behind her apple-green eyes, clear to her tender soul. Using her cane and tiny steps, she inched onward, passing Bernice on the deck without a word.

After Bernice directed four cars on board, Randolf called her into the cabin. She took a seat with them at the wooden table where Randolf's mystery novels lay scattered, Annie's plump, pink hands on her lap, the hook of her cane squeezed onto her forearm.

Randolf continued the conversation they'd been having. "There's plenty of coal diggers rusting on the banks. Steamers. Easy enough to rig one for diesel. Gas even. Then we build her a deck."

Tilting her head to read the title of a novel, Annie pursed her lips, cheeks bulbing. "That's not what concerns me. I already have a mechanic stripping a digger downriver." She looked up and waited, canting an ear at Randolf for when he'd finally glean the problem. But he only stared back.

Annie scanned picture postcards tacked to the cabin wall, then spoke in the same soft voice she'd used in class. "Anyone I've approached thinks ferrying is just stretches of boredom among occasional turns of the wheel." She looked at Bernice. "All the men I talk to." Then Annie grinned, rare for her, so full of heart was she that the preoccupation of her right thoughts and deeds left little room for expressions.

At that instant, Bernice realized where this was going. Flattery lit a smile until her fitful conscience snuffed it. Her arms and hands went numb, heedless of her command to touch her chin to posture thinking this over, that she might buy time while Annie waited.

She could move her head, though, and so diverted her gaze out the pilot's window. The posts that suspended the hogging cables appeared dun in the shadow of gaining overcast, the river depthless, Berry Mountain hulking over the scene grayly robbed of its greenery. Then came the paradox: she saw all the paintings she could ever make while certain they would never be.

Maimed now to her neck, she feared her lips would be next. So against the tide of her blood, but in the spirit of all reason, Bernice drew in the musk of the river and said, "Yes, I will ferry for you."

~

In the vaporous glow of the floodlamp, the river crept onto the fore corner of the deck where it had tilted as the ferry snagged on the weir. When the water reached a hoof of the nervous horse, she reared her sheening front quarters, Ezra still holding

her neck. With a shuddering bray, back on all four feet, the mare
bolted across the fallboard and plunged into the black water of
the channel, dragging the braked buggy until the front wheels
dropped off the edge and the horse's traces halted her. Ezra fell
from her shoulder-first with a splash and glump against the submerged stones of the weir. The mare reared again and stumbled
on her back legs as she turned for the rippling, shallower water
where Ezra lay. When she came down, he let out a groan—eerie
and protracted like the distressed sound of a foghorn.

The younger Amish men ran to the fallboard, and Ezra's
Becca screamed his name, carrying out the *ra*, which bounced
like a skipping stone across the water before it drowned into the
distance with its last lazy plods.

∾

The mare, crouching in the channel now, water up to her
shoulders, fought the whiffletree as though breaking sod. Randolf cut the idling engine and radioed a mayday. To whom?
Nobody monitored that radio anymore.

He went to the deck where the women and two older men
pulled back on the rear buggy wheels. The others were wading
to the weir, quiet and calm. Their black coats humped over Ezra
where he lay lifting his face out of the water. One of the men, his
arm probing under the surface, said, "Shin's broken." Another
took the halter and murmured to the horse. No urgency to any
of this, even as the mare rolled her eyes there with no view of
land, ears swiveling for Ezra's voice.

Telling the women and elders they'd never hold back that
buggy, Randolf went to the porch railing and took up the anchor
and its loops of hemp rope. A shift of the ferry would yank the
horse onto Ezra and the men helping him find footing with his
good leg. Then the craft would surely spill into the blackness, jet-
tisoning a buggy tethered to a gone-wild mare. The ankle-deep

river water Randolf stepped through on the deck's starboard fore corner stung to the bone. He made a hopping motion without lifting his feet; the ferry did not move. He looked to the twins on their bench, stiff of eye and limb. "Get to the cabin," Randolf said. Then he told the women to do the same. They ignored him.

He dropped the anchor overboard. Little it would do to stay the ferry. As he knelt to tie the rope to a belaying cleat, the cold of the water sucked into his knees, curdling his blood to a slush that filled upward to his shoulders and spilled into his arthritic fingers. "Tie this off," he called to the two old men who stood now by the cabin door. "And get me up."

One started away to help Ezra onto the deck. The other, feebler than Randolf, limped over, ignored the anchor line, and put out a hand. Randolf pulled him to his knees. They knelt, shaking their heads like penitents until they crawled to a post of the snubbing line. Randolf clenched this as much with his forearms as with his hands. He drew himself upward, his bones dead-heavy as the Amish man clung to his waist and the wreckage of them wobbled from the floodwater.

Shivering, Ezra stood one-legged on the deck with a man bracing either arm. Behind them, the horse—still hunkering—jerked her head side to side against her reins, searching for Ezra. Then the frame members creaked, and the ferry shifted, yanking the horse's rump so she struggled in sidling resistance until halting in an uneven stance, left hooves on rubble at the base of the weir, right in the channel.

"Cut the traces," Randolf said.

Two flat black hat brims canted as the crutchmen watched Ezra, his hat adrift, wet blond hair gleaming in the floodlamp like an October moon.

Impatience snipped sharp Randolf's words. "There's no getting that animal back on the deck. If this ferry washes away, it'll pull her off her feet, and that buggy will go with her. She'd drown tangled in her own riggings."

Ezra stopped trembling and looked into the pitch quiet of the storm's wake. "I'll not send that horse out there."

Randolf pointed at the younger of the men supporting Ezra. "You'll wade with a flashlight to the town side. Find someone with a motorboat to come for these people."

"That's a half-mile. I can't even see lights."

"It's a cold half-mile," Randolf said. "Trace the water breaking the weir. Take your friend." He turned to the dimensionless night, the nil he'd tried to breach with words and sense that last time he'd been out here, whose indifferent silence enraged his heart and made purposelessness of all.

≈

Bernice would train for two weeks. Within days though, she felt ready, the irascible current tamed against the wheel, the arc of her crossing more a road in the river than a scheme.

From behind her, Randolf called out points on the far shore to align between the stanchions of the passenger porch. "Steady ahead," he'd say. Or, "Hard to port." Reaching around Bernice, he'd let the wheel spin loose against his palm, then seize it lest she oversteer. At times, she'd avert her eyes from their course to study that hand, so unlike hers—Randolf's stained from the grease of gears and bearings, tensely ready. Beings themselves that monitored the engine through the shudder of the windowsill or told him with the touch of a belt whether it needed adjusted. They gauged by the wheel's resistance the heft of current against the rudder, tallied ferry fare. How, she couldn't help wondering, might she measure in them?

Their hands did each have in common a calloused finger—his from guiding rope, hers from holding a brush, softening though. And gone were her stains, which had been the colors of the river.

After the first week, he left her at the wheel while he read his mystery novels. From a chair beside the stove in which they burned wood chunks on chilly mornings, he occasionally called out her course. Looking over her shoulder, Bernice found he did not lift his eyes.

This made her think of crossing at night, which she'd have to do in the fall, and on her last day of being coached, she asked, "How do you do it in the dark when the fog hides the lights of the far shore?"

He did not answer. She turned to find him smiling at her. And she understood that learning to navigate by sight was only to teach her to navigate by heart.

❧

The part she couldn't practice loomed as the most perilous—getting by the other ferry. Randolf knew that if they simply passed side to side, the upstream ferry's wake would affect the other's course, and therefore its likelihood of making the landing. So he came up with a maneuver that involved them meeting at the apex of their arcing routes, the pilot coming from town turning and aiming directly at the starboard of the other. Randolf had calculated that the front fallboard of the ferry from town would miss the other craft's wooden paddles—though within a breath in the slowest current—and more importantly, miss at nearly a right angle across the yet narrow wake. This way, each ferry would continue while up-current of the disturbed water of the other's paddlewheel.

Their trial attempt would also be her first solo at the wheel—she in the new ferry, which they'd run together a few times during her training, he in the one called the *Otter*. She was glad the daybreak trip from town more often hauled mail, papers, and packages than it did people. But no doubt Randolf would be passing freighted fully with four cars and an audience of nosey passengers.

In the darkness and to the put-put idle of the old bus engine that powered the converted coal digger—christened the *Scaup* by Annie, a duck lover—Bernice waited on the empty deck, must of fresh-cut pine planks nipping in her nose. She would depart at the moment of sunup. At the same time, imperceptible in the fold of the far shore, but sure as the river current, he would be setting off to meet her.

Beneath the dawning, satin half of the heavens, a narrow gauze of daylight finally crested the mountain beyond town. Adept now at working blindly, Bernice untied the ropes and went to the wheel. She shifted the ferry into gear, throttled up, and hit the floodlamp.

Progress was imperceptible against the slow flow of the river; she might have steered a floating log. Trusting the current as her source of bearing, Bernice held her course slantwise. All those days at her easel, attuning her senses to the steady sweep and sound and scent of the water—learning it by more than sight so she could better know the sight of it—had been an exercise for this. She minded the distance off the port, alert to a light appearing out of ashes of evening that pooled in the river valley, the light by which she'd gauge just the time to turn cross-current toward it and watch the other ferry pass before her bow—she hoped.

With word spreading of a second ferry, whispers had begun about how the peculiar first mate, that girl in trousers—worse, sometimes denim overalls—was to be a pilot. As the *Otter* materialized behind its floodlamp, Bernice heard loud and clear the comments above the paddle slaps and engine drone.

"There'd be the ferry girl," a man said. "Better give the woman-driver room, Randolf."

Laughter.

All the more to aim for, Bernice thought. She swung her bow at their broadside, and the same voice let out a "whoa." Another said, "What the hell . . . ?" The ferry loomed immense, stark against the uniform background of the silvering mist.

Hats and chins extended over the porch railing as she neared. None of the passengers reacted beyond jerking back, remaining now as silent and still as the collective breath she could see them holding. Bernice squeezed the throttle knob, her other hand sweaty on the wheel, and she plowed on. By her trust in Randolf's competence, she defied her impulse to steer from seeming collision. The only satisfaction she took in the audacity was that the power of her faith was as strong as his proficiency.

Clear as her view was from the pilothouse, she couldn't have said whether the fallboard of her ferry brushed the other's deck, so closely they passed. If it did, the mounting lap of the *Otter's* paddlewheel had hushed the sound before *glump-glushing glump-glushing* into the murk of dawn like the wing flaps of some weighty bird.

Then, solo in a hushed middle place of nickel river and mist, oddly relaxed, she realized they hadn't seen one another.

◌

Near shore, Bernice turned the ferry upstream and cut power to the paddlewheel. She worked the oar to drift the rear fallboard into the landing—neither ferry had a reverse gear. Making fast a mooring line from a ring on the dock to a cleat on the fallboard, she watched a car parked in the lane to the landing. A man wearing a brown suit and with a red feather in his fedora leaned with his elbows on the hood smoking, a woman in the passenger seat. Beyond the car, Amos, the Amish egg seller, waited in his buggy.

She smiled and waved them on. "There are two ferries now," she shouted. "You can board."

But the man at the hood shook his head, drew on his cigarette, and looked across the river.

Bernice understood. She trotted up the gravel incline, much more gradual here on the eastern side where a fertile floodplain bounded the water. The man flicked away his cigarette and tipped his hat at her.

"You'll have to move your car," Bernice said, "so the other passenger can board."

The man turned to Amos with a raised brow that asked, *would you really?*

"Amos," Bernice called, "can you get your buggy around this car?"

He clucked his tongue, tugged the lines, and eased the buggy through the greening weeds and grasses along the gravel. Quiet and still as his horse, Amos would be her only passenger either way that long day and for more to come. No one else would cross with the ferry girl in the overalls and men's leather gloves she'd bought in her father's store.

After a week of lopsided ferry loads, Annie Schultz came to ease concerns. She simply sat and read on the *Scaup*'s porch. Her presence grubbed up a solace she must have known stayed in a person from those difficult days of primary school when everything new was terrifying except the comfort of the surrogate at the front of the classroom. Passenger by passenger, folks compromised pride for the convenience of the additional crossing.

As much as Bernice tried against it, she couldn't help a flush of her own pride, especially that first day Annie didn't show, and the passengers boarded nonetheless.

But a greater dilemma than falling into their same sin of pride was figuring which was more vain: the pride itself or her desire to quash it. Wasn't that just pride of a higher order?

∽

Many years later, when Bernice and Randolf finally broke away for a summer vacation, they sat on a bench at sunset on the deck of a tour boat plodding up the Hudson, having spent an afternoon at the Metropolitan Museum of Art. The river was remarkable to Bernice in that concrete abutted it and buildings cradled it where she had known earthen banks and mountains. As Randolf scanned the skyline, he spoke with an unabashed pride she'd never heard from him; it overshadowed the rest of her trip. He told her that in every challenge the river threw at them, she had proven his equal. She was perhaps the better ferryman. He held her hand where it rested on her slacks and went on to say that the most astonishing part was how her way of ferrying was completely different from his and that he did not understand it.

When he finished, Bernice tried to decide if he was proud of her or himself the mentor. Again, a quandary of pride, for she wondered if it was vain even to consider this.

∽

One morning in July, hearing the other ferry approach, she looked out to find he'd left off his floodlamp. The next morning, she did the same.

That first, almost invisible passing was memorable in how she handled it as a matter of course, navigating by the undulation of his plowing nearness, the heightened laps against her hull. Where she would have predicted trepidation, she performed with the confidence of a faith unconsciously amassed with each voyage.

But a passing, seen coming or not, was a reminder of separation. Her growing competence only strengthened the polarity of coworkers moving in opposite directions. They were united in their skill at keeping apart. Yet the river had reconciled opposites. She felt it in the rhythm of their passing, convinced that a Bernice could not maneuver past a Bernice, a Randolf past a Randolf.

～

A month mulling that she'd seen more of Randolf when she had a different occupation, Bernice began to worry that it might not worry him. Until a midafternoon in August when she caught him starting off from the town side without either of them having swung out a white door—their signal that one or the other had passengers and would be departing. She followed him with binoculars and confirmed he came alone, holding to the channel along the weir. At mid-river, he stopped. Straining behind the eyepieces, she saw Randolf drop his anchor. Then he went to the edge of the fallboard, facing her. He waved. She let down the binoculars, stunned. But of course, he would know she was watching.

Tricky steering, it would be, pulling up to him, a snub to all the forces and tendencies Randolf had addressed in devising their routes. And what of the passenger she turned to find boarding, a farmer in his pickup off to sell corn in town? She untied her ferry without a second thought.

The channel deepened near Randolf. Upstream and just ahead of his bow, she angled into the current and throttled down to tread water, the corn peddler watching in his rearview.

Hands reflexively rocking the wheel, she held the ferry by wagging the oar like a finning carp while she leaned toward the window to hear what Randolf had to say. Instead, he hopped breast-high into the channel and waded over. Bracing her deck, he drew himself up and came before the cabin window, river water puddling at his shoes.

"You never put out your hand to wave," he said.

"Don't you think you're swatting flies with torpedoes," she said, laughing, "abandoning ship mid-river to tell me this?"

He looked away, and she followed his eyes over the slow current, its faint dimples and eddies like floating cups of sunshine.

"We have plenty of daylight this time of year," he said. "After work, I mean."

Her ferry was inching toward the weir. The farmer craned his neck out his window to call her attention to it. Bernice watched the current and feathered her throttle, alternately jogging and drifting the craft. Randolf's stiff expression, his preoccupation with pressing water out of his shirtfront, told her he was nervous. "Yes?" she said. When he remained silent, she feared he would not go on, would say it was nothing.

Finally, he tipped his head upstream. "I wonder if you'd like to pole out to an island." He indicated one of the amorphous splotches of trees that seemed to rise from the water with no land beneath, the midday glare washing from the river birches their olive color. "With me, I mean. We could have a sunset picnic. Watch the herons."

She exhaled, her face easing into a smile. But when he said, "You could bring your paints," the smile tensed away. Her forearm flinched, and she rushed the throttle and lurched the ferry—as much as a ferry could lurch. Randolf braced the sill. As Bernice throttled down, she looked at that ready hand, recalled it on the wheel beside hers—where she no longer needed it.

The farmer opened his pickup door, eyes framed in the rearview. "Can't you do this on dry land?"

"Got to go," Bernice said.

Randolf nodded, not quite looking at her, then turned away.

"I'll wait for you at the landing," Bernice said. "Tonight."

He looked back, grinned.

"But no paints," she said.

◈

The river started freezing early that year—the first week of December—and soon after, in the days preceding their wedding, fitful winds that attend an even sharper swing in weather tore at treetops and downed wires.

The couple had planned a small affair; the only guests would be their parents, Randolf's brother still at home, some cousins, and Annie Schultz. Neither had mentioned it to the regular passengers, who knew them only individually and may never have guessed a romance. One of the cousins to Bernice, a high school senior she was not close to, and the brother nearest Randolf in age, who painted houses in Harrisburg, were to stand for the couple at the ceremony at Bernice's church. Then the wedding party would drive north to the bridge to make the forty-mile one-way trip for dinner at Randolf's home across the river. It would have been the first the parents met. But the cold winds exasperated Randolf's father's emphysema, the lights were out at the church, and the roads were treacherous from blown snow and downed branches.

Instead of postponing, which would have been more of an inconvenience to the minister than getting on with it by candlelight, Bernice mustered her cousin the day of the wedding while Randolf, who'd started out before dawn in Annie Schultz's Buick, managed to return from Harrisburg with his brother. They stopped for Annie on the way to church, arriving only ten minutes late. So the couple was married that afternoon in a brief and soft-spoken ceremony, minus Randolf's parents and the other brother, the rest of the cousins, and a wedding dinner.

The winds whipped fiercely that night, and snow licked westerly across the ice crusting the water's edge, and still across the grass-flats and onto the highway in the places it coursed closest to the riverbank. Randolf had offered his brother the couch in the couple's new apartment, but he'd been polite enough to decline. And so they'd set off, having to move along the drifted highway at a speed agonizingly slow for Randolf. He knew that every mile would be even more treacherous and protracted on the way home, the wind sowing snow across the windshield, flakes icing, abrading the wiper blades which left only low semi-circles to peep through.

⤳

Still in her wedding dress, for it was much too cold in the apartment to change, Bernice went downstairs and shoveled coal into the potbellied stove that warmed their rooms in the upper story of this two-stall carriage house. Because Randolf would have to pole across to his ferry every morning once the weather broke, they'd taken the closest available rental to the river, off the alley behind the broad sugar maples and stern, clapboard Georgians lining Front Street. It was necessary to heat the place from the dirt-floor bay to prevent the water supply from freezing. No need for a floor register—the gaps between the floorboards let in what warmth didn't sneak out the loose edges of the stalls' swing-out doors. When they ferried in the cold seasons, they'd have to leave the faucets dripping.

Bernice pushed shut the stove door with the tip of an iron poker, a pitted and rusty four-foot frame-bolt from an old river tug. She rubbed grit from her hands, tugged up the skirts of her gown, and mounted the plank stairs that sliced the back wall, crouching as she neared the top where she thrust open the trapdoor.

She sat on the edge of the bed until her breath quit misting, then undressed to nothing, her every nerve erect in the chill, her skin goose-bumped, and her heart beating as erratically as the wind worried the windows. She draped the chiffon train of her gown over the lampshade to subdue its ocher glow. Then she burrowed into the sheets, crisp and cold as hoarfrost, pulled up the quilts, and waited.

⤳

Thrill and trepidation can turn bitter when the excitement is for naught. Bernice had left her makeup on and hair pinned, hoping to appear just as she had on the alter. She fought tears lest she spoil her mascara. Hours later, her neck ached from holding her head just so on the pillow—a morbid, not matrimonial pose, she thought. By the time a watery white dawn seeped around the blinds to breach the lamplight and foretell one of those mornings that remain dimly uncertain about awakening, the wind had ceased. It occurred to her this was the solstice, and in her heart, something shifted, bleak as the pendulum of the hemisphere swooning onto its nadir.

What was it? All that came was a hollow pang of being too late for something. And at that, she could not hold back the tears.

&

Later that morning, Randolf found Bernice trembling in bed. He thought it was because the coal fire had died. Kneeling, he reached beneath the quilts and took her in his arms. With the hummed conviction he'd planned to impart in bed last night, he told her how much he loved her. She lay rigid and distant, and Randolf thought certainly she was not angry he was late. He kissed her with the unexhausted desire that had impelled him to walk seven miles from a snowbound car, frigid in a suitcoat and pants as permeable as a window screen. She responded limp of lip. He peeked and saw her eyes open and absent.

At last, Bernice told him she did not know what was wrong. She just didn't know.

&

Bernice woke early that Christmas to southerly gusts, a dampness in the air heightening the odors of sulphury cinders and old engine oil drafting from the floor of the stalls as she stepped from the bedroom.

She jotted a note and put it on the night table, then took her clothes to the kitchen and dressed in jeans, a blouse, saddle shoes, and gumboots. She pulled on a tan sweater, plucked her Peter-pan collar from its neck, and snugged into a blue and white, thrift shop varsity coat, its chafed leather sleeves crackling like popping corn as she swung up the trapdoor.

After feeding the stove a spadeful of coal, she mucked toward Main through an alleyway of ashy slush and mud. Leaden, rain-spitting strands of cloud scudded beneath heavens glossed in a pearly, high overcast.

Bernice crossed the silent street to her parent's neighborhood of square clapboards. With every glimpse of her hands these past few days, something caved in her chest and sucked away a heartbeat. All the while, she'd felt a tugging at her pant leg, a beckoning to her bedroom there ahead in her family's house of peeling white paint.

She and Randolf had gone to church the night before. Wanting to be alone in that home, on this morning, she'd come while she'd known her parents were at services.

Inside was as clammy as outside—her father turned off the heat at night, no matter the temperature. But the place smelled warm: Christmas Eve ham and evergreen and the lemon extract her mother mixed into cookie icing. She wiped her feet and went upstairs.

Her room was bare but for her bed and the writing desk with its drawers of oils and brushes. And, of course, the painting on the easel—that painting unfinished at the precise point she'd abandoned art.

She went to the window, drew away the curtains, and looked back. The creamy light of the high sky fell flat onto the scene.

Just a misty river. Lifeless. A thing empty and pining for its soul, like a vacant backdrop in an old-time sepia tintype.

Sitting at the edge of her bed, she looked out at the neighbor's identical home, its identical window reflecting her own. What had happened?

She tried to still her trembling hands. Instead, as if tourniquets loosened at her wrists, the quaking crawled up her arms and across her shoulders. She remembered losing whatever her heart had conceived in that moment of creative bliss. She feared that her gloom, an uncanny echo of the painting's mood, would not depart.

Bernice rose from the bed and stripped its blankets. She took down the painting and folded the top sheet around it. Then she put it in the closet and left the house.

⌒

After a mumbled discussion on the deck, the Amish men chose instead Daniel, the older of the two who'd helped Ezra out of the water, to wade for help. Alone. They told Randolf—without quite looking him in the eye—that they would not cut the mare's traces. As if in answer, out at the perimeter of the floodlight, she heaved her ebony breast upward as she scrabbled for the top of the submerged weir stones. The timbre of her whinny pierced Randolf to the marrow—a horrible sound, not rich and resonant and outflowing as the voice of a horse should be, but a hollow dirge that expired abruptly at the wall of night. The Amish men jerked their heads that way, struck by the strange quality and conciseness of an utterance they otherwise knew to resound between barn walls or to peal across the hills from fields and roadsides.

"Hurry," Randolf said to their messenger. "For God's sake, hurry." Daniel started away, and Randolf leaned out from the deck until the flashlight beam diminished into the blackness beyond the paddlewheel.

He returned to the cabin and stared alternately at the night and Ezra's family on the forward bench. Ezra's Becca supported his head on her lap, his body stretched and shivering under a tarp of sailcloth while the swaddled baby lay asleep upon the thighs of the twins huddling against their mother's other side. It would have been a picture of tenderness, washed in that nimbus of irradiated mist. But this was an isle of light lonely and suspended on a storm-angered river, poised to break away and fizzle at any moment like a dying star.

෨

One evening in November, she stood by the sink of their two-cupboard kitchen, which always smelled of Ajax, and waited for Randolf to look up from the mystery novel he read at the table. Even for reading, he used a hard-backed chair—a preference, he'd once told her, from his Navy days. Lately, her thoughts and feelings, clipped and scattered and hard to get hold of, had been like downy feathers in the wind. She concentrated on the moment, couldn't contain a smile when he set down the book. "I'm pregnant," she said. She closed her eyes a moment. The single note of a hum sounded from deep inside, a strummed bass chord. "I mean, I'm pretty sure. Fairly."

Expressionless, Randolf looked to the window over her shoulder. Bernice knew he compared months of gestation against those of the next ferry season. Pent hope and fear curdled in her middle while she waited for him to say something, maybe embrace her.

"August," she said. "It will be an August baby."

He nodded. "Well," he said, and he picked up the book.

෨

Staring out where the floodlight ceased against the nil, he pictured that window, conscious now as he had not been then of the night's invincibility, impenetrable as black marble. His understanding of darkness was obscured in those days by figments of a creamy kitchen light and a coal fire beneath his feet. It troubled him that it would have taken seeing what lay hidden by his hardened heart to stopper the pink joy he saw wash from her face. But that would come only after an instance of anguish, the black silence hemming his consciousness like ghost wolves carrying in their fangs the inevitability of obliteration, grumbling in their breasts things unsaid, things undone.

Oh, God, if it really were specters—something, anything—he could let it be. *Be.*

◦

He told them to don the lifejackets stowed under the hinged bench seats. The elders, standing on the deck, refused them; none fit the children correctly. For the next hour, Randolf remained at the wheel staring past the swiveling ears of the oblivion-bent steed tethered to this floodlit ferry, this chariot of fire. Even at such a miserable prospect, his spirit—collapsed upon itself—couldn't so much as lift a sigh from his breast.

All at once, the horse and seated passengers turned their attention in the direction Daniel had gone. Randolf knew they heard what his aged ears could not—the motorboat.

The sharp beam of its spotlight breached their bucket of illuminated haze. Seconds later, the boat's wooden hull scraped against the ferry, and Daniel boarded. The man at the wheel, town constable Tom Dietz, tied a mooring line from the boat's gunwale to a deck post.

Dietz did not like Randolf. As long as there'd been ferry pilots, lawmen had held the notion they were complicit runners of fugitives and contraband. Worse, a step onto a ferry was a step into murky jurisdiction. The magistracy of a ferry stuck in the middle of a river was particularly undecided.

Randolf had more than once rationalized the river as a place exempt from the law, a middle sanctuary where one might winnow trouble out of a situation. While earlier generations of Susquehanna ferrymen had witnessed escaped slaves or crate-toting bootleggers, he'd known shoeless kids lugging buckets of strawberries to sell on the town side, berries picked in the dark. He'd seen nervous teenagers crossing on Friday nights to meet coal diggers' daughters they were forbidden to date. He'd turned blind eyes to deer out of season, to battered wives in flight with children. He could tell in a glance whether a stranger was a nostalgia buff, river romantic, or nervous runaway.

But there was more with Dietz. Years ago—in fact, during Bernice's pregnancy—Randolf had broken from his typical reserve and rallied a group of petition-signing, meeting-attending ferry supporters to persuade the borough council—or all its members except Dietz—to revoke a resolution endorsing highway funding for a bridge across the Susquehanna. The campaign affirmed the democratic process, though in an odd way. For despite the district's good state legislators having acted on backroom appeals by highway department bureaucrats to stage-manage the council into signing the resolution, in the end, all they wanted was a measure of their voters' support for or rejection of a bridge. They'd subjected themselves to bureaucratic wheedling by habit, not collusion. A revocation by popular demand was better than the resolution—they could brag they'd abided the peoples' will. All because Randolf had opened hearts to something even he'd taken for granted.

The fight hadn't been all about his living—he could have made more money and worked fewer hours at the machine works. Instead, as he attended borough meetings to learn about the bridge, he became more and more incensed at business owners and local know-it-alls jumping in with the same vague and ready platitude any time he challenged the council for grounds in backing the project: "It'll bring growth."

Refuting that would have been easy against people idiot enough to be waiting maids for career-padding Harrisburg bureaucrats who couldn't give a rat's whisker whether the oldest, least obtrusive transportation system in the state, not to mention one efficient and undeniably romantic, disappeared. The ferry gave the town identity. People—tourists—visited town *because* of the ferry. And even if they didn't, the bridge would net no gain: families on the other side were not opting for a neighboring community to shop for cars or groceries or to visit doctors or dentists; there *was* no neighboring community for them. But because Randolf's passion had increased in proportion to his recognizing the river as its own being, he would not dishonor it by lowering the argument to mere economics.

He'd never credited a place as existing beyond his consciousness of it. What he'd thought of as nothing without him, he'd been nothing without. Seeing the river this new way, he could paw it not only with rational thoughts, but his heart, and so defend it with a fluent imagination—a part of himself he'd rarely regarded. Throughout the ordeal, he tapped a well of eloquence that bypassed his brain, impulses flowing from his heart to his tongue when he stood at meetings, to his pencil as he wrote letters to the council and newspaper between ferry runs. The river was speaking through him.

At one meeting, frustrated over the refusal of grown people to think on their own and doubtful the council even looked at his letters, he stood and read from one, his words rasping through his throat as if they'd grown bristles. His neck knotted, his forehead burned, and looking up between phrases, Randolf saw chins around him and at the council table edge toward this uncharacteristic show of emotion.

"A river is the music of a rippled current," he read. "It is its own atmosphere, a condensed universe of fish and invertebrates and diving mammals."

He stopped, stuffed his letter into a pants pocket. "Bridges snuff that sound and the cool musk of the water. They make rivers silent flat snapshots. But worse—" he glared at the council— "your bridge will be one more brick in the wall of denial that separates us from remembering we're no better than what we come from."

"Sure," he said, nodding, "crossing a river by ferry is not quick. But inconvenience is adventure. That's why we're better off than those who have bridges. We still experience the drama of weather and the hazards of hydraulics."

He pointed toward a window. "That river connects us to more than our world. Paths have crossed at our landing for as long as people have forded or paddled birchbark canoes or pulled cable rafts from there. It's why this town is here and how you come to be in this room at this moment. What will we lose by breaking that connection?"

Randolf paused there. Years later, he would look back convinced that a premonition made him stop, a warning that he was trading a bridge for some great loss to come. He would be certain that at that moment, he'd felt the future, as certain as a river, coming from what had been, ever flowed to what would be.

☙

He didn't win over the throng, rather diverted its witless drift. As word of his attempt to save the ferry spread, people who actually deliberated ideas attended the meetings. They seconded Randolf's assertions, and like the ducklings to the duck, the crowd veered with the momentum.

Afterward, estranged from his father-in-law—a man whose daughter Randolf had led to a livelihood of ferrying—he understood Bernice's reticence about the ordeal. It hadn't been misgivings limiting her to mere smiles of empathy as he expressed frustration or rehearsed remarks, rather pained restraint.

And he came to see that when he'd embarked on the campaign, Bernice had helped him, albeit with the subtlety and obliqueness typical of a woman making a gift of herself. It was she who'd freed the pool of thoughts and words, her liberating gesture a simple one: finishing that painting she'd started the day they met.

Sipping coffee at the table one morning, he found she'd hung the painting on a wall in the sitting side of their common living area. It drew him to his feet and across the room. There he was, poling his canoe out of mists framed by water and mountain. The scene seemed as much in him as he was in it, Randolf not subduing a current, not crossing an obstacle, but a man in concert with the place. And while the composition's beauty was that it could not be whole without him, Randolf felt something dire in this.

He would look into the painting often, feel this dilemma that owed to something other than the competing light of the two windows between which—for whatever reason—she'd placed it. The scene was obscured to the point he'd squint to take it in, through his eyes and to his heart, all thought unnecessary to give his self up to that utter illumination of the river's being. And he told himself that a presence he felt in the spaces unoccupied, from which all the painting's elements and meaning flowed, rectified the beauty and dread.

As time went by, Randolf was surer of that. And it had to do with his first impression. Though he knew as much about art as he did spelunking, his reaction that morning had been that this painting, which he'd last seen on an easel wet and unfinished, was as complete as a painting could be. Art, he sensed, was only an effort, never an accomplishment, repeated attempts at something we, Tantaluses all, were bound by lot to reach for but never grasp. This paradox, though, was as much a sentence as a blessing—a kind of sour medicine which, Randolf thought, was dosed out again in the final message of every painting of worth painted, every book thoughtfully written, every dance danced from the heart. It said we're obligated to seek truth so it can remind us of the law that we're too minuscule to know it, moral order binding humans to live in constant pursuit. In this, that we could not know truth, was some answer to the dread.

Having no artistic bent, Randolf arrived here thanks to peculiar instants on the ferry when, lulled by river chatter, he was overtaken by an interplay of light and mist so intense it stupefied his senses. Unable to rein the experience into reason, he could not put into words what strange wonder he'd touched upon, a gift that was as well an admonition.

Many years later, he took the painting down from a wall in the two-story home they'd bought along the riverfront. He'd decided the night before to hide her work forever, having encountered this power in a new way. Out on the river, where he'd once thrived in the absence of light, he'd faltered, and that would be his last time ferrying until Warren Stewart came to see him about transporting the Amish wedding party. Randolf's soul, drifting desperately as a message in a bottle, had careened into an abyss of grief that in his chase enfeebled him, striking a bedrock of obstinate throes so deeply isolated from the outer world he'd attuned to over his 75 years that he'd been insensible to them—the quaking fibers of a now aged and broken heart. Breathless, he blasphemed the severity and bitter irony of an admonition that could also be a gift, the darkest, gravest of all admonitions.

∾

Randolf approached Constable Dietz where he rested his boot on the deck's gunwale while he stared into the jaundice haze cast by the floodlight. Dietz was a paunchy, expressionless man in his sixties, his uniform just a pair of blue factory pants and an off-white button-down shirt, pens and a glasses case jutting from the pocket. He wore a gray-plaid derby with the brim turned down across his brow in the Dick Tracy style. Ignoring Randolf, who couldn't stopper the thought that his victory for the ferry had cursed him, cursed so many, Dietz looked over at the horse and shook his head. He pointed to the others, then his boat. "All you Amish get in."

Becca removed Ezra's sailcloth blanket while he sat up, Randolf stepping over to help him to his feet. But Ezra, his hands bracing his shin, would not stand. "One of us is staying with the horse," he said.

Only because Dietz's whisper came out more a hiss could it be heard against the gurgling of river water through the deck planks. "I don't give a damn if that horse drags this jumble of lumber to Harrisburg, you're all coming with me." He glanced at Randolf. "Except the brilliant skipper who marooned you on the weir."

One of the elders spoke up, but Dietz raised a hand. "Remember who polices buggies as much as cars in town. You'll be wheelbarrowing your apples and cinnamon breads if I hear from you again, Miller or Yoder or Stoltzfus, whichever cousin you may be."

When Randolf finished helping Ezra onto the motorboat, Tom Dietz came and stood so close Randolf could see the black pores that stippled Dietz's nose. Dietz watched Randolf a moment, finally looking down at Randolf's shirt buttons. The slightest smirk creased Dietz's eyelids. He shifted his weight to one leg, wriggled his hands into his pockets. Randolf remarked the deliberate nighness, the posture of leisure in the presence of teetering menace.

Dietz looked up. "Would have done to have a bridge."

～

A baby dead in the uterus, the doctor had told them from his desk before a window in the only four-story building in town, might be delivered unrecognizable, a decayed pulp. Not knowing how long it had been deceased, he could only say Bernice would go into labor within weeks, at which point it was critical to get to the hospital.

"How?" Randolf said. "How did the baby die?" He looked from that impassive face to Bernice. But he saw that matters like this did not come from hows and wherefores. They lay beyond the tendency to vanquish all into the known. As if something to be solved.

It was easier looking at the doctor, stolid in either professional detachment or coldness brought on by years in the occupation. After a moment, he gave what Randolf considered an indirect reply, which he later regretted having taken as the comfort of control he'd sought in a rational explanation, his wife quietly witnessing the vanity. As though he could command the wind, turn a tide.

They would need to study the baby, the fetus, the doctor called it, for "defects." Then he could predict the chances for future stillbirths. And so the matter was pared down safely to something tractable—the question of what to expect should she become pregnant again.

There was another way. The doctor's words dropped onto his lap in monotone blocks, detached, indirect, final; the obligatory litany of options and risks. "We could operate. Sometimes the mother chooses Cesarean section over delivering the fetus."

Distancing Bernice to the third person eased Randolf. It made objects of the dear subjects, laboratory specimens hedged into the human domain, tidy as abstract numbers within the confines of math.

"The condition of the mother," the doctor went on, "and whether she wants to have children again—"

Bernice cut him off. She would deliver, bring forth what they had made together, what had swum in the womb to her joy.

◈

Silence saturated the damp after-lull of the storm, stopped abruptly at that incessant purl of water against wood, the paradoxical, forever, bubbly shushing. Even the horse was quiet, at least to ears dulled by years on alert for irregularities of engine noise.

After switching off the light to save starting power, Randolf felt his way back to the deck and peered out. The pendulum of night had descended to its black nadir. He wished for the horse's pant or blow, a splash of her shifting upon the weir, racked every nerve for something beyond the tireless river. Damn the nothingness.

And then, as one now and again tunes to a ringing in the ears, he caught the conversation that bandied endlessly in his mind, the troubling riddle he couldn't let go. A conversation about nothing. He fumbled about near his waist, found the guy cable, and squeezed it, a corrugated, cold snake tense in his hand.

◈

One morning at the kitchen table, he'd told her he heard voices come up from the river. Not that snivel at the nose of the ferry as it plowed across the current, audible against the engine drone by its sheer persistence. Instead, spirits spoke—or so he thought—those of all the people who'd crossed at that point between mountain passes, ferry route for 200 years, ford well before that. Confluence of souls, reservoir of their leavings.

He used to think that if he listened hard enough, he'd decipher the murmuring, his head trembling with the intensity. But his labored breath confounded concentration, an effort as fatiguing to the brain as to the body. Even in later years, after he'd apprehended the nothingness besetting all, he believed that voices called—the only difference was knowing they could not be immortal. Waning echoes maybe, which like everything else, did not matter. Still, some vague familiarity in that babble kept him listening.

She had surprised him by dismissing the idea—he thought she'd be the more inclined to accept spirit voices. But over the years, recalling her words, he came to see she was acknowledging them.

"They're nothing," she'd said.

He was about to sip from his coffee, the peaty aroma from the halted cup dampening his brow, watering his eyes. "Nothing is something I cannot comprehend," he said.

"See," she said. "You've admitted nothing is something. But it's everything. Nothing is everything."

It was a puzzle, a play of words, but he could not let it go.

༄

Damn the nothingness, the laughable vanity of groping in younger days for eternity in the infernal natter of a river.

Vanity. His greatest of that sin swelled into his throat, depriving him of the old, thin consolation of whispering out against the gloom. If he'd realized the pointlessness of all, maybe he wouldn't have fixated on lost income and replacement pilots. All at the expense of giving her the one thing close to mattering. When it still might have. But only after devoting every free moment to locating, meeting, and being turned down by retired coal-diggers, then composing weeks of one-vessel ferry schedules, had he thought to comfort her as she lay in bed through even the waking hours abiding the womb-tomb of their child.

An aftertaste of that unkindness lingered ever since, as bitter to his conscience as the river's flow of shadowed memories parading the wilt of her body against the current's song of *shush, shush, shush*. He knew she'd too seen it. Perhaps with a bit of tenderness from him, the luster of her hair and skin may not have dulled by the week. The crystal complexity in the depths of her eyes may not have dissolved, their color eclipsing as a starless twilight steals by degrees the blue of the sky.

And so damn the river too, damn the ferry. They had cost a child. Then they had taken a wife, Bernice never again the same. She shouldn't have been at the helm afterward, for a residue of stillbirth remained. Keeping her at work, he'd made her contain the pain—it smoldered instead of burned out, smoldered and left caustic ashes in the center of her being.

She was as suited as he to the river but not to be on it. And still, the more she declined over the years, the more Randolf immersed them in the business, convinced they could make a good living only if they one day owned the ferries. Owned this piece of the Susquehanna.

He turned an ear, rubbed his useless eyes. A sound had breached the murk of memory. His mind scrabbled through the last moment. The horse had been gasping. There—a strained intake of breath, spooky, human-like.

The aloneness, absolute and heavy as this night, pressed in with the weight of watery depths, the rhythm of his breathing broken like the horse's. Even in the first days, fresh grief wringing his insides, he never called for her except in bewildered whispers. Now the name ballooned in his throat. The harder he fought to stifle it, the more it tried to rupture his windpipe. When he could hold back no more, his cry came out so forcefully he could have shaken the heavens—were heavens up there.

∽

Though the ice held off that winter, it was the coldest he'd known. Not a steely and piercing northerly cold, rather perpetual dampness. The real cold—the dangerous cold that hung in fog, seeped into bones, waterlogged hearts. Hers.

After twenty-plus years, they'd bought the business. Annie Schultz had died, and her sons and daughters, scattered between Harrisburg and Philadelphia, had been eager to part with it. Bernice was silently neutral during his excited reasonings at breakfast every morning. He factored in there was some money—their parents, gone by then, had left inheritances. Her father's building brought in monthly rent, though a meager one, operating more as a knick-knack shop, overalls and dusty tools from his reign the only things that could qualify it as a dry goods and hardware store. Her reserve only increased Randolf's resolve. Or so he'd thought; looking back, he realized he'd been persuading himself, not her, the mirror of his conscience. He wouldn't recognize that owning ferries added nothing to the kind of life they wanted.

Annie never would have sold the business, and he believed now that by the wisdom of that kind heart, she knew that operating *and* owning it wasn't worth the toll.

Passenger traffic continually declined, especially during the fair-weather months—that season from which they borrowed their living the rest of the year. Commercial shipping shifted to trucks too heavy for the ferry. And drivers of air-conditioned automobiles from the farming side began perceiving it easier to go forty miles out of the way for hardware or groceries than park 15 minutes for a one-mile ferry crossing, allying with the townspeople who'd supported a bridge and had never since stowed their pride onto the ferry.

Fueled by ever-cheaper cars and gas, farm folk eventually drove even farther, to doctors and shops up in Selinsgrove or down in Harrisburg, rather than to the town they could see from the riverbank. With that, their trade of local produce moved in either direction; had it not been for the Amish, Randolf and

Bernice would have retired one ferry long before her sickness. Back when he'd already been telling himself that just owning it was enough answer to its existence.

So for a few added dollars, they ferried further into each end of the colder months, the dwindling riders primarily school kids visiting friends, and Amish. The couple stopped only when the skeins of ice along the shore were too hard on the hull, then resumed after the last big floes came wheeling upon the treacherous fury of snowmelt surging out of the headwaters and bending the river birches on the drowned islands.

To cut costs when they couldn't ferry into twilight for fear of trees awash in the higher waters of the shortest days of March, they moored her *Sunrise* and ran together on the *Sunset*. How those crossings differed from ones on slow summer Sundays when Bernice would come aboard while Randolf kept the wheel. Back then, she'd stand motionless at the fore of the deck, a trouser-wearing, bob-cut swashbuckler, cheeks set toward adventure in an indulging grin. Though she figured into the view no more prominently than that breeze-bristled slate water and malachite mountainside which had facsimiled themselves across his eyes, the whole valley thronged to Bernice, as water converges and pushes at the inlet of a sluice. The scene called to Randolf's mind her paintings, and that always brought a pang of sadness, the river coursing her without that beautiful transformation. He knew now the toll that had taken, the want and sacrifice in only feeling, not revealing, the mystery of that middle place.

On their partnered March runs, Bernice drew like a frightened turtle into the sleeves and hood of her parka, nestling against Randolf to keep warm and never putting a hand to the wheel. He would have liked a break—those crossings made for difficult steering, the ferry veering when the paddlewheel's drive belt, cold-stiffened like the bones in his fingers, slipped against its pulleys. And twenty times a day he'd have to endure the ache and burn of those fingers as he untied ropes and oiled gears. Lazing around the landings between infrequent trips only added to the paralysis, made him cross, for Randolf hated waiting, a reminder of idle days at sea when he'd go stir-crazy, heart fixed on returning to this valley.

He read her heavy slowness as indifference, his foul mood intensified by thoughts he knew in his heart, but would not admit, were cruelly unfair. Why dillydally, of all places, right beside him? If she wasn't going to help, did she have to be in the way, shrinking and shivering? Shivering until she stuttered out a sigh and went and huddled in his chair.

Randolf had scolded her for God's sake, said she'd better not loaf when piloting on her own. He'd judged it all a weakness of will.

Between those longer seasons, they had only the rawest days for maintenance, starting before daybreak at the moorings on a bank of the old canal. There had always been plenty to do: engine rebuilds, decking and side-plank replacements, paddle repairs, endless greasing. The extra runs in rougher conditions made everything worse, particularly when higher waters forced emergency landings downstream of the weir. The *Sunset* was showing her age, the barn-red walls dull and mildewed. Doors and windows, moisture-logged and un-square, had to be struck to open. And the engine hacked and popped, needing a coaxing to start at all. Moving about and rubbing her hands above the chunk stove kept Bernice from shivering, and she worked as best as she could alongside Randolf, enduring the cumbrousness of what seemed never enough layers of clothes. But she coughed and coughed, Randolf ignoring the sagging crescents beneath her eyes, dim as muddy water.

∾

It turned out not to be a chest cold when she couldn't get out of bed, instead a weakened, fickle heart that made itself known by fluid pooling in her lungs. On the worst days, when he had to carry her to the car and drive to the hospital on the hill above town, she had no way of clearing the gurgling; she was suffocating inside herself.

As Bernice clutched the hospital bed's metal rails, she seemed an ocean away. Fear pursed her brow where he'd known relaxed pondering, blue lips quivering with a labored word or two. Once, she let out a child's peep, "Help," a memory clouded in shame, for he'd turned away, told himself he was hiding tears. But some brute part of Randolf had been ashamed of the desperation and frailty, not yet admitting the graveness of the situation.

Later, he'd try to dull his remorse by recalling he'd been enduring the hardest two years of his life. Seven days a week he ran the business while tending to Bernice, pushing the *Sunset* past its limits as he tried to make up for lost runs, never quite enough customers to justify hiring a pilot. Bernice languished between trips to the hospital for oxygen therapy and new medications. She never strengthened enough to want to leave the bedroom. When she lost even the wind to take the stairs on their returns from the hospital, Randolf wondered what he'd do when she couldn't walk to the bathroom, how he'd handle what the candy stripers did.

When whatever broke next incapacitated the *Sunset*, he ran the *Sunrise*. Before long, to keep one or the other operational, he was making repairs every night with a flashlight tucked between his neck and shoulder, sometimes until daylight when, grime to his elbows, he'd go straight to the wheel. If he had to run off in search of a part, there was no time to pole to the other side and put up a sign about the delay, and it was too early to call anyone to do it for him. And so, more and more customers, already impatient with irregular departures, abandoned him.

If no cars or passengers awaited his landing on the town side, Randolf ran to the house to make Bernice a meal, or he drove

to the hospital when she was there. At home, he never knew
in what condition he'd find her, always expecting he'd have to
rush her off as she lay suffocating. More than once, sleepless,
drained of spirit, he went to the house forgetting—*forgetting,
dammit*—she was at the hospital.

Friends offered help; he declined, an impulse he couldn't
explain. He told himself she wouldn't want anyone seeing her,
but he suspected the decision was not selfless.

Bernice made few requests of Randolf beyond reaching out
to hold his hand with those fingers cold and brittle as icicles. He
knew the idleness maddened every wasting muscle of that body
which, like its trapped soul, had been sprightly as a sparrow.
Yet, one soggy, October morning during her last hospital stay,
she shocked him by speaking out for something the moment he
stepped into the room.

"I want paper," she said, less gurgle in her lungs and a shine
in her eyes.

His heart, chilled as the Kromer cap damp against his crown,
flapped at his ribs.

"To draw?" he said.

She eked out a smile.

"A pencil," he said. "I'll get a charcoal pencil, too."

He should have stayed a moment, indulged in that spate of
strength. But, elated, he ran off. Fifteen minutes later, he laid at
her fingers a tablet and pencil from the knick-knack. She looked
out the window where the valley cradled the river steely and
mute. He stepped back, waited. But her eyes had lost that luster.

"Bernice?" The word dissolved into the sour silence of a mid-
morning hospital ward, the measured slosh of her respirations
just the tick-tock of eternity.

⟨∾⟩

It's austere, a person's dying, none of the pomp and circum-
stance of before and after, striking in its indifference to the stuff

of life and death. Its moment—or moments or hours—of attack cancels all the logic of the living, and so vanity. In this authority rests the black terror, the shock which begets the monster of agony that stomps and shrieks about the hearts of loved ones.

They seldom go calmly, as movies make us believe, as in hopes and imaginings. Instead, in the manner of birth, there are lurches and excretions, guttural croaks, and strangled screams—death punctuating the whimsy of all between.

Randolf would have liked to have said he'd held Bernice. But during her hour of last agonies, he clutched her shoulders, pinned her against it.

So much for a peaceful passing. So much for a note from which to move on.

◈

Had the horse not answered with a screeching whinny—ghoulish, the sound of darkness could darkness enunciate itself—Randolf would have been insensible to the moan that his anger over the folly of all had lifted out of the constant queasiness in his gut.

His mind turned to a dead cavefish he'd once seen drifting in the current, washed from its underground tributary. A small white thing, helpless-looking, what with scales grown over the bulges of its eyes. Living in double darkness—blackness all around while blind even to that—the fish was lucky not to have believed in the mask of daylight. For what advantage was sight against the finality of nothingness?

Randolf thought about that, infernal hope stirring an objection—what if it was the other way around, daylight the reality as he'd assumed in that life before glimpsing this other side, in what he thought of now as naivety. A splish of water, faint as lips smacking, called his attention to the horse shifting, to the otherwise incredible, silent patience of that creature, scared as it must have been. No, he decided, it was *not* the other way around, for something can't hide itself with nothing, like this indomitable nothing could hide itself with something. And he couldn't help a sick satisfaction at that, a twisted I-told-you-so.

He canted an ear. What now? Something out there roused by their outbursts. He listened, strove as that fish must have when it tried to make its blind eyes see beyond its overburdened sense of smell. A voice, satin-soft as the sheen of a moonlit river.

Nothing. Nothing is everything.

Randolf turned in a circle, reeled. He firmed his feet, spun the other way, a tear coursing his temple. The words tumbled over themselves, inside his mind and out. Had something answered that cry for her? Or was his imagination acting on its own? He had to know if it came from within or out there.

The voice melded into his thinking. He uttered the name, this time a question that he hated hazarding, delivered so tentatively and papery he might have addressed someone in a church pew: "Bernice?"

His answer came as a mustering of the darkness, the amorphous mother blackness coalescing into the shape of the fallboard at his feet, the hogging cables descending in his periphery, the bust of the black mare. She'd squatted deeper, immersed again to her shoulders, head reared, hind legs likely tangled worse in her traces from the water's relentless rush—an omen of an unmooring, when the river would finally take her under.

The sharper the edge of that silhouette became as darkness tugged down the pale fringe of its veil, the farther the voice receded.

"Stay," he said to the night. But now, the full form of the ferry gathered around him.

A glimmer appeared in the mare's lacquered eye—the light of dawn, its source still imperceptible to Randolf.

She was looking out at something. Randolf followed the stare, but that animal eye saw better than he. Then he caught the shine wavering—the mare was moving, stretching her neck toward whatever lay out there, and so Randolf racked his eyes, the horse letting out a whimpering neigh.

There *was* something downriver—vague and indefinitely shaped to Randolf's inferior eyesight as a puff of smoke. The mare began to struggle, her forelegs stumbling against the weir.

The ferry shifted, and Randolf's "No" turned her urge for whatever she saw to panic. She splashed against her traces, lost her footing, and plunged deeper, submerged but for her muzzle pointed toward the dawning heavens.

Randolf couldn't reach for his jackknife, for the ferry pivoted on the weir, throwing him onto the deck. A shadow, even in this shadow time, fell like the wing of a raptor as the tethered buggy toppled. He rolled away as quickly as the burden of his years allowed, slamming his head into the fallboard beam—all that stopped him from tumbling beneath the veering ferry as a wheel snapped from its axel, and the rear of the buggy crashed so close, it hemmed Randolf against the beam.

Ache racking his skull, he squeezed shut his eyelids. The ferry swung until the stern aimed downriver and took the motion of the current. The drag of the drowning horse kept true their course, a heavy and steady rudder, she was.

Forcing open his eyes, Randolf tottered to his feet. The Susquehanna stretched now visible to each shore. Dull slate sister to the morning sky, she lay palisaded by black borders of equidistant treelines. Oh-so-slowly and deliberate, the ferry continued along the very center of the river.

The middle, the point of their passes, was a place of harrowing moments when adrenaline enabled swift-water maneuvers he couldn't have repeated otherwise, steely fingers of death goosing his flesh. Now they seized him—not a cold and quick clench as he would have expected, rather a feverous, increasing squeeze that wrung out all sensation except malaise, even the pain in his head turned to a kind of nausea of the brain.

But for this sickness and the weight of age and fatigue, he'd have cut the traces, started the engine, and tried to limp the ferry to shore. Reaching into his pocket and touching his jackknife, eyes fixed beyond the invisible weir, out at that receding place where he and she had met halfway, he dwelled on that. No, it was something else. By the other part of age, the wisdom, which was just as accursed, he knew there was no use.

How many passes? How many years?

Swirls agitating the ferry's wake in nearer water drew him back. A black hoof broke the surface, plowed along, wagged, and disappeared. He'd rarely known the river so deep and swift— she'd more often been a gentle companion, even in her moods.

Now he could save neither his ferry nor the dignity of that mare. Her destiny was sealed at a broken buggy axel wedged tight where the deck and fallboard hinged, Randolf able to make out that he couldn't reach the traces to cut them without plunging into the fast and frigid Susquehanna. He stroked his knife, his thumb brushing a scrap of paper worn soft as tissue, and looked up at the sky. All that remained of the clouds was a mist.

A memory of that gauze of half-water, half-air skulked in. He felt the old horror the painting had conjured when he saw himself merged with the elements. An answer to that, he recalled, was in his minuteness—which wasn't too hard to feel right now. But that had been in relief to the hint of something beyond his comprehension. He'd found comfort in ignorance. Now that he was up against his reckoning, he wasn't too sure.

Water rushed against his shoes. The drag of the horse had offset the flat, the ferry submerging before him at the starboard. The chill from the river reaching his ankles slid along his backside like rods of steel. He guessed this stretch ran ten feet deep in the flood—if an immersed corner of the deck caught on a rock, that was enough hydraulic force to rent the ferry into the pieces he'd built it from.

A moment later, up to his knees, the aslant deck and the weight of the current testing his balance, Randolf saw the light of the motorboat crossing along the drowned weir. To the searchers, the blot of the ferry, dimmed by the mist and with no light of its own, might have been a drowning island.

The ferry lurched, and Randolf crouched. The cold Susquehanna, lapping at his thighs, slipped its fingers beneath his hide. He fought shivers and watched the motorboat finish tracing the weir, go still, then zag downriver, some reluctant crew of townsfolk hunting too slowly for what swept deeper into the muddy depths.

A prevailing wind whipped Randolf's cheek. It shouldered into the superstructure, helped the river take another gulp. He shook his head side to side. Invisible meddler—always wreaking some devilment or the other.

She told him once she'd loved painting the wind.

"How do you paint something invisible?" he said, though he felt the wind in her paintings as surely as he did the mountains.

"You paint the invisibleness. It shows the parts you see."

Then she said it again, the riddle: "Nothing is everything."

He chuckled.

But eventually, he agreed invisible forces were a paradoxical necessity, as guiding as they were resistive, so he'd not opposed them, instead navigated by them. And not just the winds of the river, but of marriage, of life. There'd be no navigating or marriage without wind. Everything needed its antithesis—that's what bore it out.

So had he come out here this last time looking for her and found some opposite?

The hum of the motorboat broke the burble and ooze of water eddying around the sinking porch posts. Dropping to his knees, the river up to his middle, Randolf waded backward and hugged the craft's tallest member—an upright that suspended a hogging cable. Was it higher than the river was deep?

The chill washed to his core. He stopped shivering and knew that was bad. Then the hull collided into one of the river's infinite boulders. It dipped then scraped along until going into a sharp pivot, timbers screeching and groaning, Randolf being sucked under as he took a gagging slug of river water. The current lifted his legs, and he had hardly the strength to cling to the post, not a second's breath in his lungs. All sense of bearing befuddled, he begged his legs to flail for the deck, but the panic of the breathlessness undermined his command of muscles that, stunned by the frigidness, had already been defying him. The ferry took him deeper. He had no fight. And just as he found the presence of mind to realize that if he let go, he might bob to the surface, the ferry quit turning, and by an excruciating exertion of willpower that knifed through a brain throbbing already for want of oxygen, he made his legs kick. His feet found the deck, and releasing from the post, he sprang upward, head breaking the surface and lungs devouring air.

On his toes and up to his chin, he reached for the upright. But his hands no longer worked. So he clasped it with the crook of an arm as the cold Susquehanna paralyzed his limbs, making him powerless to swim, and he was terrified at the agony of drowning.

The hull had about-faced on its fulcrum rock, pointing him downstream. The buggy had let loose, it and the horse adrift or snagged out there. Next, the ferry would go, either to the bottom or the mercy of the current. What would happen to him was a matter of whether he lost his arm-hold before or after. If before, he'd be swept—drowning—downstream. If after, he'd collide into the cabin and perish beneath the ferry's porch roof. Then wash away.

The cold was jellifying his thoughts, his wits going the way of his slackening grasp. Forcing his head to turn, finding the superstructure immersed to the tops of the cabin windows, he caught a red dot angling across the water. Emerging from a veil of mist, the motorboat took shape behind its port light, and as Randolf creaked out a call for help, the motor revved, and the prow swung his way. But upon the blurred bellows of distant hollering, the ferry pitched from her mooring and cast him off.

In the terror of release, he gasped—an underwater gasp. His lungs flooded, his throat and head wanting to burst. Only by spontaneous convulsions did Randolf wiggle to the surface. He strained to devour air—futile paroxysms of neck muscles—and as the torture of suffocation ripped every nerve, his crown struck a stanchion of the porch roof.

Down he went into the Susquehanna. And all was black.

∽

In that river crypt, Randolf remains. As does a folded piece of paper he sometimes carried in his pocket. He could not have said what spurred those occasions that he picked it up from his dresser where he'd kept it since that day he figured out how they would cross from opposite sides.

Though just a simple pencil drawing, it diagrams the physics of their feat. First, the lines for the riverbanks trace each edge of the paper, the one to the right marked T for the town side. Within them, in the fashion of an arrow, two pencil strokes move diagonally toward one another. Each terminates at its own small rectangle, these indicating the ferries, the rectangle from town aimed at the front of the long side of the other. A gap no wider than the tip of the pencil separates the rectangles. But separate them it does.

At times he'd take that paper from his pocket and unfold
it. He'd focus on the infinitesimal space between those bodies
moving toward their opposite shores, never quite to touch. Not
quite. Something about that void washed warmly into his shame
and repentance—and there was much of that. It was a distance
that, paradoxically, perfectly unified. There a river came from
what had been, going to what would be, and he'd smile with a
moment's contentment that was forever.

NOT 2B

Lucas inched his hip across the number painted in red on the door panel of his car as two boys stopped behind the trunk. He reached into his jeans pocket for a pen.

The shorter boy said, "What kind of candy you got?" and tugged the brim of his hat, embroidered with a neon-blue 7C.

"Peppermints," Lucas said and slid along his car to the quarter-panel, clicking his pen as he nodded at the yellow plastic basket on the trunk. "Key chains, too."

"No Tootsie-Roll Pops? No Kit-Kats or Snickers?"

Lucas shook his head and shifted his backside into one of the dents he hadn't gotten around to pounding out. He looked away to the other street-stock racecars parked down the front stretch.

"So who are you," the boy said while the taller one studied his autograph card, brushing away bangs the color of muddy water.

"Lucas Ogden."

"Never heard that name." The boy lifted onto his toes to see the knitted key chains, blue with red 2B's, spread over the trunk. His friend scanned his card again, then leaned out to see the number painted on Lucas's door panel.

"Won two heats last year," Lucas said. "Starting ninth in the big race tonight."

The shorter boy shrugged. "You never won no features. I'd know. And how come you got a B in your number? There's none in your name."

"Just like the sound of it," Lucas said.

The other boy pointed at his autograph card and whispered. Under the brim of his cap, his friend narrowed his eyes at Lucas. Then they turned and started along the clay of the front stretch in the direction of the late-model racecars wedged diagonally in a row along turns three and four, tail-ends backed up the banking to the white guard rails, noses canted toward the track apron. Their hoods cast a smoky luster in the sulfur-yellow track lights, their fresh polish occasionally cackling out the bright colors of sponsor's logos as camera bulbs flashed from the fans lined up to shake hands with the late-model drivers in their racing suits, get their cards signed on autograph night.

"Hey, kids," Lucas said as loudly as he dared before they got beyond the next street-stock driver. "You wanna sign my car?" He stepped back along his door panel, reached into his pocket for a magic marker, and tapped the red 2B. "Go ahead, right on the number."

The taller boy turned his head enough to look at Lucas with one eye, swept back his hair, and spat. Then the boys laughed and ran into the flow of fans who paid Lucas and his blue and red racecar no more than cold glances, who sometimes let out sing-song calls of "get a bath" or "Lucas-loser, the boy killer."

To win tonight, Lucas thought, looking up at the moths that for this one evening a week had their halos of glowing track light to flicker round and round in for all their glory. To win this one—it being autograph night. It being the big feature.

When the track announcer called five minutes left in the intermission, Lucas put the knitted key chains into his candy basket. A loud bunch waited across the track beneath the flagman's stand, where people squeezed back to the bleachers through an opening in the fence. One of them aimed at Lucas a hate-edged holler that pierced the air right out of him, even before he caught the meaning: "Ought'a paint that 2B black."

None of them faced Lucas's way—six or seven skinny men in their forties, gray sideburns, pocket t-shirts, cigarettes in hand, all gasping raspy, drunk laughs. All wearing hats with neon-blue 7C's.

One of them looked upward, eyes diverted just past Lucas with that oblique challenge of rival animals. "Oughta just drive a hearse," he yelled, screaming the word hearse. Their dry snickers lit laughter through the throng at the fence and caught a spark on the other side, igniting like ether up through the stands that mounted the coal-spoil piled against the highwall when this place was a strip-mine.

Lucas pitched the candy basket through the window opening. Someone yelled, "Long live number 7C," and hoots and catcalls erupted in the bleachers. Lucas lifted his worn and dusty sneaker over his door panel, grabbed the tubing of the roll-cage, and pulled in the other leg. As he slid into his seat, he switched his ignition.

"Goddamn," he said when the engine did not turn. "Goddamn that starter."

◈

Lucas sat there while the other cars fired and drove over the bank of turn four to the pits. When he waved to the wrecker for a push, Lucas heard over the fading engines the laughter of eight-hundred Saturday night race fans.

Fanning his clutch as the wrecker pushed him along the backstretch, Lucas couldn't catch a start. But no way would he let them send him to the pits without firing the old girl, not tonight, no goddamn way. So he stayed in the turn instead of coasting over the bank for pit road. The wrecker kept on his bumper, the driver showing Lucas the finger over the dash the whole way down the front stretch. And that put the crowd on its feet.

Without a helmet and with the engine dead, he could hear them yelling, "Loser Lucas," "Dirt Bag," and the new crowd favorite, coined by College Boy, "Wrecked-em." And he couldn't help glancing up through the windshield screen to see them all, ladies and men and little boys and girls from every double-wide and farmhouse in the county, holding up seven fingers. And that slanted, neon 7C, leaning forward to look fast and determined, eyed him out of the oblivion that resurrected and reared over him every week here, eyed him from t-shirts, ball caps, and banners, squinted out from a picket of limp flags up on the lip of the highwall where beer drinkers sat on tailgates and lawn chairs, the flags rising from poles planted in the stake-holes of their pickup beds.

The engine finally caught at the end of the front stretch, and Lucas got on it, swung the car sideways in the turn. He kept it open on the backstretch, headers coughing, then cackling in that bursting roar of acceleration that blew the garage doors off his grinding life as Lucas Ogden the body-man. But as he braked in the turn and made that sharp right over the bank and into the pits, the rush faded, leaving a throbbing awareness that his solo hot-lap had just called attention to a bad starter and the shoddy shape of this old LeMans, that he was his own sponsor, quarter-panels and hood advertising no patron Harley dealer, no trucking company or bank, not even a gas station. Just Lucas's Body Shop, the only car out of the hundred in all the classes here tonight that needed a push start.

Cathy had wanted him to change the name to Lucas Body Shop, said there was something stupid about Lucas's, made it sound as if there were more than one Lucas. But hell, he'd had the detail shop make a hundred red decals for the quarter-panel.

And it wasn't like there was a sign out front of the garage to match.

Down over the bank, the pit flagman blocked him from driving to his row of racecars parked behind their trailers. He walked around to the driver's side and pointed a rolled red flag at Lucas's head. "No helmet," the official said, "and you make a hot lap out of a push start." He put a hand on the roof and leaned close to Lucas, who just stared ahead, keeping on the gas, sure to hold an idle.

"Lucas," he said, his words a slow, deliberately hissed scolding, "I'd disqualify this heap, except that so many people—" he lifted his chin at the wall of spectators blazing up out of the track lighting—"want to see your filthy ass beat, this being Benjy Chesley Memorial night."

Lucas gave more gas, smoothing the engine's chug-pop, chug-pop, and he let out the clutch just enough to hold the revs while only inching along, steering down his lane and turning in behind his pickup and trailer, which wasn't a trailer, just a two-wheel dolly.

He revved the engine, climbed out, and ran to lift the hood, then pinned back the throttle linkage with the paperclip he kept on the floorboard to make sure she kept running when this happened. She'd been burning oil lately, and he ignored the scowls and head-shakes that the smoke and noise drew from the neighboring pit spot's drivers and actual crews—family and friends who came to work on chassis adjustments and engine tuning, came to cheer from the fence during heats and features, wore their driver's printed t-shirts.

Lucas wished he could say something, but his whole face twitched against the impulse to tell them he couldn't let the car stall, that he had to run his feature tonight. Had to.

He started along the length of his car, running his fingers across the body, strumming creases left where he'd pounded out dents, most of them the intentional bumps he'd taken over the past year, shots by any one of these drivers. It was nice before—back when he'd been invisible around here—except to Cathy. She'd come with him every Saturday night, his one-woman crew and cheerleader.

No, there wasn't any talking to them. Just get back there and put your head under the hood. He'd keep it there as much as possible until he could go and shake it all off in that whirlwind he came here to ride for the admission price of all the looks, all the names, all the fender shots and spins they could muscle on him.

But first, he wanted to look across the way.

And before he reached the back bumper, he saw her. There, sitting on the trunk of College Boy's racecar. She'd been watching him, reclined over the rear window-opening, legs spread, arms over the roof like it was living room furniture.

She pulled on her cigarette.

Lucas couldn't help the wave, just a slight lift of his hand no higher than his waist. He immediately reached to push his glasses up his nose, as if that's what he'd intended.

He looked away to where men and boys ran from pickup beds to racecars, carrying tires, monkey wrenches. Groups poked heads under hoods, ass cracks smiling back. Damn, she looked good. Lost all that weight since she left him, did her stint as track trash. But now she'd latched hold of College Boy, shined herself up like that car, sparkling with bracelets and earrings, necklaces, the way College Boy's car did with all those big-deal sponsors painted fender to fender. Just how the hell did he get a Budweiser sticker on there?

Lucas glanced at her again, then toward the track out over the open hoods of racecars on jack stands, making out to listen to the lineup for the novice-class feature coming over the P.A. At the edge of the back-and-forth movement of people in the strip between the cars, he caught Cathy slide off the trunk and cross toward him.

"Lucas," she said, loud enough for anyone nearby to hear while she stayed at a distance out on the roadway. "Robin Kline tells me that for autograph intermission, you went and put out those key chains I knitted last year."

Lucas shrugged, still looking toward the track. The lights silhouetted the number 7C backward through banners hanging from the fence where pit people would watch the races from turn three.

"I can't believe you still used those," Cathy said.

Lucas looked at her now. "If you want them back, I still have all of them."

Cathy huffed out a laugh, lifted half her top lip. She glanced at the black smudge coughing from Lucas's exhaust. "So you're really going to run that feature tonight."

Lucas squeezed his hands into his jeans pockets. "Why not?"

"Why not?" Cathy laughed and rolled her eyes. "If you haven't noticed, it's Benjy Chesley Memorial Night." She waved a hand end-to-end across the pits, then up the bleachers. "How many 7C's do you need to see around here?"

Lucas always saw 7C's. He saw them in the liquid red numbers that blinked on his stove clock, in tree limbs out behind the house when he fed the dog, saw 7C tangled in crossing plug wires under his hood and in the crinkles of customers' fenders. He read it in the pages of his JC Whitney catalog at the kitchen table, in from the garage for a ham sandwich. 7C materialized out of the fizz of dots when he watched channel 10, the way numbers came out of the colored bubbles the eye doctor leafed through, way back when he went to those appointments. It spelled itself out in the Cheerios he ate for supper; it floated in the toilet bowl Sunday mornings after an evening of too much Jack. And every night, Lucas watched that fast, forward-leaning

7C do its laps in the pinks of his eyelids, which he closed against the bedroom light he left on during his sapping, whirlwind, sweaty, almost-but-never-quite sleeps.

"I have to run that race," Lucas said.

"If you think it's gonna somehow prove it wasn't your fault, Lucas—"

"They don't care," he said.

A novice-class car lurched along the strip to line up for the next feature. Cathy stepped out of the way toward Lucas. "Look around, Lucas. They care."

"No, it doesn't matter to them whose fault it was. People just need someone to blame."

Cathy tugged at her jeans pocket while she took out her cigarettes with her other hand. "You're so stupid, Lucas."

The jeans were so tight he wondered how her cigarettes didn't crush. She looked like a different person, had a figure under those pants now, something he'd never even considered when it hadn't shown. He thought about touching her, just touching her. The reality that he hadn't touched a woman in the year since she'd left him hadn't felt so raw as now. He looked away from the hip-huggers, from the t-shirt with College Boy's car number swelling out from breasts he'd never given any thought when they were lost in a larger body, until now when there was a difference to tell them by.

"Do you want them back?" Lucas said.

"What?" She sucked her cigarette, drawing the flame of her Zippo into the tip.

"The key chains."

Cathy snorted out cigarette smoke, clapped the lighter closed against her hip. "Holy shit, Lucas. Are you ever stupid."

She looked at him a moment. Lucas pushed his glasses up his nose. He liked that she wore eyeliner now. But following the sharp edges of her eyelids became too personal, private, making

Lucas think of her and College Boy, and he pulled his gaze away as if it were the hand he'd wanted to touch her with.

"Keep the key chains," Cathy said, turning away. "And try not to kill anybody out there tonight."

Lucas watched her start toward College Boy's yellow and red Monte Carlo. She trotted to stay out of the way of another novice-class car, the creases under her back pockets snapping back and forth with the pointy thrusts of each hip.

Damn, she looks good, he thought.

∾

While most of the pit crowd walked up the bank to watch the novice-class feature from the fence, Lucas kept under his hood. Over and over, he checked the hoses, pulled on the throttle linkage, listening, wondering about the oil burn. Mostly, though, Lucas was thinking about a tire, the driver's-side front tire.

He went to the bed of his pickup, sifted through a bucket of tools, plugs, and bolts, and pulled out his tire gauge.

Back at the car, he bent to the tire and twisted the cap from the stem. Letting out air sharpened the memory of that day the tire blew. He pushed the nail of his little finger deeper, wanting the air out as quickly as it would go, as if the hiss of it was a fresh searing of that incident against his heart. He couldn't help feeling the sudden veer of the car as the tire gave in turn one, or remembering that if another car, a lap down, hadn't been on his quarter, he'd have come around, spun right there, been done with it.

He'd never run better, racing his way to second in a feature, and he'd been reeling in that 7C. Then the blown tire slowed him in the backstretch, pulling the car hard left. But in turn three, he realized he could get on it—deeper than before—and still hold the ass-end right at the verge of swinging around. His best guess was five laps to go. Making better time in the turns, he thought he might be able to pull it off.

Benjy Chesley was a kid of sixteen who'd torn up the local quarter-midget series. That had won him a nice ride here in a car owned by a garbage hauler—a racing fanatic who'd lost his son in a street-car wreck. The fans loved that kid, good-looking, always wearing his hat backward in the pits. The track people loved him too, for he brought in a lot of high school kids, sold lots of t-shirts. It's all about the t-shirts, he'd overheard College Boy once say, bitching as usual about the state of racing.

They were all nuts about Benjy Chesley. And no doubt the kid could drive.

As usual, out front that night, Benjy Chesley's well-financed white and blue racing machine hauled. But with bad luck turning good for Lucas, he had something for him. By the time Lucas came around to where the tire had blown, he knew he was making better overall lap time. Hell, he hardly had to cut the wheel to take the turn, just brake once, hammer it, and steer hard right to hold the rear from coming around. Best of all, with the flat tire pinning him to the bottom of the turns, he could move under cars where they slid up the track—lapped cars, maybe the kid's car.

And he did nose up to Benjy Chesley, right before the flagman showed two laps to go. But that tire was tearing, and like so often happened in the life of Lucas Ogden, his only advantage tugged at his weakest link. The tighter the flat tire let him take the turns, the more the car wanted to spin, pulling at the tire, trying to tear it from the rim. If he could just get the car under the kid.

Then, in turn three, coming around to take the white flag, he nudged his nose in there, got inside his rear bumper for the straightaway. There were lapped cars ahead, but so long as Lucas kept beneath the kid down the front stretch and over in turn one, he'd get past him by the backstretch, and that checker wave would be his. He dared flinch a look at the pit crowd lining the fence. And there was Cathy, clawing the chain links, shaking them like she was going to break through, face red with her cheers.

He kept his nose behind Benjy Chesley's rear tire down the front straightaway, the white flag waving. But it wasn't far enough for Lucas to give it full gas without losing the rear-end when he motored through the first turns, trying to get good acceleration to take the kid. He'd have to wait and try to get farther under him, entering turn three.

Lucas's front bumper in Benjy's quarter-panel gave the kid enough to work on to keep them both slow, and Lucas slid his nose up to the door when Benjy let off for the turn at the end of the backstretch. With the inside advantage, Lucas knew now he'd pull onto the front stretch with the lead. But for who knows why, a lapped car was slow in the middle of the turns, almost stopped, and there was no way Lucas and Benjy Chesley could run the turn, sliding through it side-by-side, without a wreck. And truth be known, though it never would, Lucas let off the gas.

∾

He pushed the tire gauge onto the stem. Six pounds. He'd never run less than eight, even after learning the advantage of a low left-front—just too much risk of popping the tire off the rim. But tonight, he'd take that chance.

So he let out a little more air and gauged the tire. Five pounds.

The cycle of engine hum from the track faded as the novice-class cars finished their race. Street-stock drivers, crews, kids, wives ran down the bank to their racecars while the late-model hotshots in their fancy red and white race suits strutted away. As the beat-up, dull-colored novice-class cars spilled past them from the track, the late-model drivers passed Lucas's pit spot in pairs, cool and easy, arms crossed, talking about the clay conditions, bitching that tonight's extra-long street-stock feature would tear apart the track for their finale.

Lucas paced behind his hood, waiting for line-up, frowning in turns at the black smoke puffing over the trunk from his exhaust and at that left-front tire. He went to his truck, got a Slim Jim from the seat, and bit off a piece as he leaned over his engine. But he could hardly chew—his teeth seemed hollow, brittle, his head and arms and legs light and airy, as if all the churning in his gut had sucked the marrow out of his bones.

He reached for the throttle linkage to rev the engine and saw his hands quivering the way they did in the garage when he tried to weld body panels after a string of especially bad nights. He pulled, the engine gnarling in that gritted-teeth way that always splashed life up out of a puddle glinting somewhere in the basement of his memory. The growl gnawed at his spine until he heard a voice on the P.A. When Lucas let off, sharp cusses pierced through his idle, firing at him from drivers up and down pit road.

Then over the *pop-clack, pop-clack* of Lucas's engine, the P.A. boomed: "And folks, would you please rise."

A driver standing with buddies in the bed of a nearby pickup—a 7C banner draped over the rear window—yelled: "Shut that piece of shit down for the boy that can't."

Lucas bent his head farther under his hood, ran his hand into his hair, where it caught in a shag at the top of his skull.

As if the announcer could hear Lucas's disruption way up in his booth in the middle of the stands, he roared into the P.A., "Ladies and gentlemen, please bow your heads." Then he changed to the soothing, even tone of a funeral parlor greeter. "Join me in a moment of silence for the boy we remember with our special thirty-five lap feature, the Benjy Chesley Memorial Street-Stock Race."

Lucas straightened from under his hood, pushed his glasses up his nose, and, glancing at the loudspeaker hanging from a light post, realized that every hat brim in the pits was aimed his way. Of its own, his arm stretched toward the driver at the next pit spot—Mason, one of the Dixon Brothers, leaned against his quarter-panel.

"I, uh—" Lucas pointed under his hood. "I gotta let it run. My starter."

Mason flinched his head back, then looked away, embarrassed.

It was the moment of silence now, and to break it even by running to Lucas's car and killing his idle would be an act of disrespect to Benjy Chesley. Lucas knew he'd take at least one hard shot for this.

He sidled to his fender and, after the announcer thanked the fans, got on a knee and poked his thumb into the sidewall of the left-front tire. It was soft, like the gel of flesh his jeans pinched when he tugged them up his waist.

∾

Twenty-four cars, a thousand to win. Lucas knew it'd be a hell of a mess. But after line-up, driving with the pack up over the bank and onto the front stretch for the pace laps, he reminded himself that fifteen of these twenty-four cars were behind him. Finishing fifth in his heat—thanks to a crash—had put him ninth. He worked his wheel back and forth down the stretch, opened his throttle to make a little noise just before the turn, and thought about what rode on five pounds of tire pressure. He had a shot at this thing. Goddamn, he had a shot.

He felt racy getting on the gas, but not in a way that came up out of him, instead seeming squeezed on him, as if the situation called for it, as if something bigger maneuvered him. He gritted his teeth to get their feeling back and squeezed every muscle from

his shoulders to his butt to reconnect his brain to his body, wanting to stop this sensation of watching a movie of himself driving a
racecar. And Lucas fought a creeping wish for racing the old way,
under the old terms. No pressure, just get out here and drive the
best he could, in a car just as good as he could build it.

The extra expectations wedged between driving the car and
the race itself seemed to diminish Lucas Ogden from the picture, a picture so big he couldn't feel the moment, the wheel in
his hand, the sweat that always girdled his waist as he melted
into the racing rhythm. He opened his mouth to taste the grit of
track dust, listened for that low bass of thumping headers as the
pack, wound and ready to release when the race started, backed
off for the next turn.

∽

They'd have to run extra pace laps for the announcer to get
through the long line-up. From the backstretch, he looked up
the coal-spoil bleachers. Packed. The place was burning with all
the electricity of Benjy Chesley neon blue. Hats, flags, beer cans
a-waving, flashers blinking on the pickups backed along the lip
of the highwall, everyone rising with the tremor that mounts
into their guts from this thrumming bunch of cars urging bumper to bumper for that explosion of engine roar released by the
waving green flag.

Then he saw the banner, a sheet spray-painted with "Not" in
blue, "2B" in red, stretched along the front straightaway fence
just after turn four. And for one of few times in his life, Lucas
Ogden had a vengeful thought. He wanted to blow around this
track of clay so fast, so furiously, he'd tear that son-of-a-bitch to
tatters and send them snowing up into the frenzy of moths and
engine rumble. That pushed away his wish for racing the old
way where he was in touch with the moment, with the car, made
him want to be seen out here near the front of the pack.

Over the front stretch, the flagman pointed the rolled green flag in the air—one pace lap to go. Lucas looked to the infield as he rounded the first turns, watching for the yellow lights, which indicated pace laps, to stop flashing on the wreckers, saw the emergency workers jumping up to huddle in circles on the giant tires. Then he caught the ambulances, one at each end of the infield, and for a flash of that moment that had no mark of beginning or end and so seemed always there, he saw those red lights flashing, saw a back door opened to his car and another to the one he'd pinned, driver's-side against driver's-side, to the rails in turn four, saw the frantic firemen at the truck tugging the starter cords of generators and running with saws to the roof, then slicing through that blue 7C, saw others squirming through the back window opening, legs out, as they reached for the handsome boy who used to wear his hat backward in the pits, his head and shoulders now convulsing with the last pumps of his heart as it surged blood out his nose, drops sprinkling at each lurching of his head as if this were some purging, spraying Lucas, spraying even the 7C on his hood. And the blood running down each car's door panel onto the track, that boy's cousins and sisters and mother and friends and fans screaming from the fence, begging they save Benjy Chesley, prince of this ring.

And then Lucas, dizzy in the crash's aftermath as the hysteria rattled and shouted against his skull, set himself free of his belts, crawled to the passenger side, pictures flashing of the kid, instead of pulling high, braking hard for that car stopped in the turn, and that causing Lucas to plow the kid's rear quarter, spinning Lucas round, slamming and sandwiching and shearing the kid's car between him and the lapped car, stripping sheet metal that somehow daggered through Benjy Chesley's roll cage, into Benjy Chesley's ribs as his car, bound to Lucas's, came to a stop along the guard rail.

When Lucas fell to the track and wiped the boy's blood from his eyes, the smudge of a fuel fire seeped from under the hood of that white and neon-blue 7C and into the cockpit, sending those firemen backing out of the car, scampering for extinguishers. Then up roared flames from the fuel cell of the 7C like some burned offering from the stricken souls, dead-still and silent in the stands.

∽

The green flag flew and had the cars behind Lucas not nosed him down the stretch, he'd have missed accelerating into the start.

Run tight, he told himself, and he cut for the bottom of the turn, aiming his bumper at the crescent of truck tires painted white and marking the track apron, Lucas nudging them as the ass-end slung out and the car swept through the corner sideways, tires a-spinning as he put it to full throttle. And as if that low tire followed a groove, it held his nose to the bottom the whole way through the turn, down in the good packed clay, while three cars slid up into the loose dirt cast there by tire spin. That low tire gripped so tight against the car-swing of full-throttle that Lucas felt all the weight thrown to the rear wanting to stretch the chassis apart while he slipped under those three cars. Then he was lined up for the straightaway, and with a sharp left pull on the wheel, he stopped the momentum of the slide and all four tires took hold, and he shot into the backstretch. Lucas Ogden was hauling down the straightaway in sixth place, in position to enter the turns low, where he needed to be.

But it took five laps to work under the next two cars, and he knew there was top equipment to contend with up ahead, three cars much better than his, with their fancy suspensions and super-tuned engines that had no leaky pistons. And every time he swung into a turn, Lucas caught at the edge of his vision, a few cars back, the glint of track lights on College Boy's yellow and orange Monte Carlo.

Lucas needed two things to run up front. That low tire had to hold to its wheel. And he had to regain the old comfortable control of the car to be where all he thought about was driving. Neither seemed likely.

And he saw the contradiction in needing to race the old way—which he'd resisted wishing for—to compete in a league beyond his abilities, his equipment. It made him even more mindful of how much he'd given to the mercy of that tire he'd tampered with.

Trouble ahead in the first turns—two lapped cars, running side by side, spinning, then collecting three others to make a parking lot of the track. Lucas stayed low and just made it through. But when he slowed on the backstretch—yellow flag waving, wrecker lights flashing—he took his first hit. Another of the Dixon brothers, Ricky, moved above him and drove into his right quarter-panel. Lucas surprised himself by how quickly he reacted. Instead of pulling away, he leaned on Ricky Dixon's car to keep him from tearing away sheet metal, which might cut a tire. Dixon backed off by the turn but put his bumper to Lucas's rear-end. Lucas glanced back, saw the finger over the dash, and accelerated to avoid getting spun.

Passing lapped cars to line up in his fourth-place spot, Lucas thought about his reaction. He'd needed that hit to get his reflexes back, to lose that suffocation that had numbed the nerves between his thoughts and hands. But he could not afford hits at race speed, low tire tugging at its bead. And even if he survived them unscathed, he'd be the one to get the black-flag ticket to the pits for unsportsmanlike driving.

The field turned four laps under yellow, then, speeding up to take the green flag, Lucas looked over his shoulder at the cars farther back, still on the stretch. For now, he'd baby that tire, concentrate more on keeping them from passing him than getting under the leaders. But fast cars ran back there, and racing out of turn two, he caught at the edge of his eyesight the orange and yellow of College Boy letting it all hang out, passing cars on the outside. A fancy chassis and new tires let a driver do that, and it would be trouble.

Somehow the race stayed clean and green for fifteen laps, hard, shoulder-wrenching work, Lucas blocking drivers from getting under him while picking off lapped cars when the field spread out. The three leaders had moved a stretch ahead when the yellow flag flew for a four-car spin in turns three and four, and Fast Eddie Reese had pulled alongside Lucas in the front stretch.

As the field slowed for the pace laps, the flagman climbed from his perch onto the track, holding his headset tight to one ear, listening to the scorers up in the press shed over the rumble of the fifteen remaining cars, which hadn't crashed or blown tires. He sorted the field by pointing and waving as the drivers passed, signaling Fast Eddie around Lucas, putting him back to fifth. Looking over his shoulder, Lucas saw a window opening full of yellow and orange and a fox's grin from College Boy.

The pack moved along the backstretch, and the flagman climbed to his stand, brushed the dust from his white shirt and pants, and pointed in the air: one lap to go till the green flag. That meant seven laps remained. Lucas couldn't waste time fighting off College Boy's outside moves and still charge through the turns to pick off the leaders from the inside. He wiped the lenses of his goggles, squeezed the wheel, and sucked fast, deep, dusty breaths. Your car's slower, he told himself, but handles better on that low tire. He laid his foot into the gas, coming around to take the green flag, riding Fast Eddie's bumper while College Boy nuzzled his rear-end hard. So remember, Lucas thought, you can't play the same game.

He sailed high into the first turn, anticipating College Boy's outside move. That slowed College Boy, leaving him to fight off the car sliding in beneath him, and Lucas went into the backstretch on his own, buying some time but already with distance to make up on Fast Eddy. How would he make his progress in the bottom of the turns while holding off College Boy above him? At least the rear cars, once lapped, were riding up along the rails to let the front cars race. They'd be in College Boy's way, at least until they saw they were helping Lucas Ogden.

Lucas lifted off the gas only for an instant now as he entered the turns, then put it back to the floor, his engine hot with that peaking grind of machinery that's about to blow. His blood boiled, churned in his arteries as if any minute it would shoot out his nose, blow out the ends of his fingers, his toes. The weight of the chassis pitching as he swung through the turns, the pulling spin of the tires, the temperature of this car pushed to its limits, they all tugged at that thin bead sealing five pounds of tire pressure.

"Hold you son-of-a-bitch," Lucas said. "Hold."

His eyesight and adrenaline heightened. It was almost like racing the old way, losing track of time and himself in the exertion of urging his machine ahead. Except that neither the car nor the stakes seemed in his own hands since he'd given over to wanting more than doing his best in a race. He felt removed from his car, shame creeping in about his success riding on something other than his own powers.

But he was moving under Fast Eddy now, College Boy on his ass with five laps to go, and Lucas shot through the front stretch fourth in a train of six cars, noses glued to tails.

When Lucas nudged under the next car in turn one, College Boy made a gutsy outside move, putting them three-wide. It called for delicacy, for all three dancers to stay in perfect step to avoid a triple spin, and it was up to Lucas to lead. He fanned the gas just so, limiting the throw of their weight, and all three came out of turn two together, tails wagging, sheet metal buckling, and finally the middle car backing off to try and nose under Lucas for turn three. But if anything, Lucas would not let any-one underneath him. He peeked over his shoulder and caught College Boy busy picking off the car on the outside.

Nose to the apron through turn four, Lucas shortened the distance to the two leaders while they swung high. Four laps to go, and those two raced each other hard in the following turns, putting Lucas in the driver's seat as he came out of turn two locking bumpers with the second-place car.

But there was more at hand than chasing down leaders with no time to spare. That orange and yellow car was right there, pushing him down the backstretch, and he knew that because College Boy could drift high in the next turn, he'd be locked on Lucas's rear-end as he kicked it up into the loose stuff and would keep pushing to spin him. So Lucas eased off the car's bumper in front of him and faked high before he dove to the bottom for the turn, and College Boy backed off.

With three laps to go, College Boy played Lucas smart, fol-lowing him right under the second-place car, running single file out the backstretch, and being patient through three and four where side-by-side lapped cars held up the leader.

Lucas held on to the car as if it drove him, could no more feel himself steer than breathe. He'd handed his body over to the big show and given driving to a desperate quarter that for a year had begged for this race, a selfish, vindictive, proud part whose moment had come.

Going into the front straightaway, passing under the two lapped cars, Lucas saw enough open track ahead to finish this thing unhindered by slow cars. In front of him, a down-stater led in his fancy black and gold Cutlass, the name of an Iron City Beer wholesaler painted across the trunk. The flagman held up a pair of fingers for two laps to go, and Lucas flinched his head and saw he had a bumper-full of College Boy. This is it, he thought, the last round of your boxing rematch. Lucas was center ring now, like a man in that one sport he used to try to catch on T.V., guys he admired for throwing out offense and dodging with defense, both at once. Take your hits and give them, he thought, but throw them better than you let them do it.

College Boy's smooth-firing engine pushed Lucas down the track so hard his front-end was light coming into turn one for all the throttle he'd gotten into the rhythm of giving. The low tire didn't stick, and Lucas was too late backing off as he cut the wheel. He slid up the track, and College Boy nosed under him, slamming the edge of his bumper into Lucas's door panel, pushing him toward the rails. But by some volition that he more watched than felt himself will, Lucas did not back off, cutting hard into College Boy. If Lucas was going to spin, the son-of-a-bitch was going with him.

But College Boy lived up to his name and backed off to save himself, and they spilled onto the stretch fishtailing their cars straight. College Boy swung back to the outside and came down on Lucas. And because Lucas did not have equal power, he turned his wheel and leaned just as hard on College Boy, hung all over him, putting a drag on that shiny Chevy, their scraping side panels panting over the high whine of College Boy's engine, the cackle of Lucas's tired 350.

With Lucas's car modified to hold low and fast in the turn and College Boy equipped to go high, they fanned apart at the corner to catch the down-stater. And before they broke onto the front stretch, they'd sandwiched three-wide, nothing ahead but a white flag waving one to go, and a lapped car in the middle of the track.

Then that front tire shook Lucas's attention, vibrating right up through the steering wheel, shimmying the whole car. She'd blown.

Center track, in front of eight-hundred people who'd come to see him lose, Lucas let out a steady, grating scream, the way he did in the garage to squelch out ads for that radio show he hated where a woman, some doctor, took calls from scorned lovers and soothed them into temporary numbness just as uselessly as a good jag of Jack did, talking down to them in her phony, butter-voice. Only now, he tried to silence how *he* might dupe himself into that final defeat of conceding it all.

He cut right, leaned heavy on the down-stater, rubbing him against College Boy—the only way he could slow the bunch. Offense and defense at once, he thought.

They went into the corner with all three hard on their brakes, none of them able to swing out his ass-end with acceleration to slide through the turns. And smothering the down-stater with all his limping weight, Lucas focused hope on the bumper of that lapped car they would close on by the final turn. One of the three would have to give—a body-man knew better than anyone the rule that two objects couldn't occupy the same space.

Rules of ones and twos sparked a thought: could one win solve two problems? Lucas only now recognized that he was even trying to solve problems, and though fighting a crippled racecar didn't leave time to dwell on that, something about there being two coaxed him to back off so he could think through what he was really doing out here.

No, he would not back off.

Hugged together into the backstretch, the three grinding out all their R.P.M.s, Lucas told that flat tire not to free itself while he leaned into the others—but not so much that he'd put College Boy into the rails. Lucas wanted a win, but a clean one.

And even at seventy miles an hour in the middle of the stretch, dust in his mouth and a car ready to crash, Lucas caught in the perimeter of this bowl of throbbing roar and light that kindled up out of these coal-black hills one night a week, everyone on their feet, hats, fingers and beer cans in the air. Out ahead, faces of racers' crews, wives, girlfriends leered from the turn-three fence. He squinted and squeezed the wheel all the harder and blinked those people out of his mind because they, he told himself, didn't have a goddamned thing to do with why he was going to win this race. Hold you son-of-a-bitch, he said to that tire rattling against his grip, hold onto the rim.

Only that one time had he gotten so close. But the nearest he'd come to feeling the glory of what he might do was imagining it through the little tatters of satisfaction that came every week trying for it, thought-free moments of contentment that were surely morsels of what a win would be like. Kind of like the best times with Cathy—tastes of some glory they'd surely get to experience. Never reaching it always gave an inkling that he needed to step away from her to catch a rhythm in getting by, to get back to those beautifully bare moments that in themselves could be satisfying but which he hadn't brought himself to admit he was truly after more than any final triumph with Cathy, with anything.

Cutting the wheel into the turn, Lucas glanced for the ambulance against the rails. At the end of a race, he always pictured it up there, doors spread wide like jaws devouring the lifeless body of a kid, the spray of fire extinguisher coating the gelled skin of his face like some greasy powdered doughnut-hole. But instead, in flashes sharp as the camera lights popping now on the coal-spoil, Lucas looked back on himself working his car through every lap of this race, frantic and removed from it, as if punching the buttons of a remote toy. He didn't feel that old trauma, focused now on winning, focused on winning those people up there in their neon-7C ball caps and t-shirts—as much as he tried not to know that—focused on Cathy pressing her eyelined face into the fence. Funny how the boy, the part that mattered, faded against all that.

College Boy was trying to pull apart and drift way up the turn to take the lapped car on the outside before they broke onto the front stretch for the finish. With his flat tire and hoarse engine, Lucas didn't have it to race College Boy if he got around that car. He'd lean a little harder, keep College Boy slow up there. Then even if College Boy slid his nose past the down-stater, he'd be behind that lapped car, which by rule had to be on the outside for the stretch—a pick. Sticking on the down-stater, Lucas would keep a bumper ahead, while College Boy, forced out against the rails, would either give to the lapped car or learn from Lucas the law of two objects.

Lucas pushed both cars up the track, and as they straightened for the stretch, he dared glimpse at the flagman. Leaning out, pointing the flag stick over the packed clay, his other hand unfurled those checkers, then snapped the bottom of the flag, holding it square in that dramatic display of *Attention, this is for you, leader.*

Lucas cut harder into the down-stater, wrinkling an Iron City Beer logo and aiming College Boy at that lapped car that moved up to the front-stretch rails. He locked on the black and white of those checks as the flagman lurched out farther, tugging at the bottom of the cloth, stepping up his little Hollywood pageant before he'd release the flag into a frenzy of figure-eights to hail the winner and ignite the crowd.

The three cars broke into the stretch, and with a bigger eruption of camera flashes, a scene popped into Lucas's mind—the sportswriter for the county paper stooping to shoot the victory picture in front of the stands as Lucas knelt alongside his racecar and held that flag out next to the red 2B on his blue door panel. Nobody in the crowd would be happy about that, including himself because there was no denying they—not his desire to quash grief for a dead boy—were why he was leaning out now like a lesser boxer, using that lapped car as a trick to overcome the limitations of his engine, his abilities, just as much as Cathy was why he wanted that checkered flag to flutter out into the roar for Lucas Ogden.

And it all seemed suddenly more things to get in the way of how Lucas realized now, supercharged in the racing rhythm, he wanted his life to be. Race, live, love under his limitations, as he accepted them by *his* judgment. That was the only way to recover from the mischance of a blown tire and piercing sheet metal, the only way not to let those things keep putting off what was necessary for him to regain the tatters of satisfaction he used to know. He needed to be a racer, not to be under the flagman's stand posing for a picture.

In that surge of straightaway speed and camera-flash and trophy lust, Lucas admitted he'd ached for redemption from that neon 7C and all those stricken souls who cloaked their emptiness behind it, painted it there on their hats and shirts as if saying the injury swelled right out of their heads and hearts. Lucas hadn't driven this car by his own powers, his own sloppy limitations, in a year; it had been driven by that mob who'd cast him out, who didn't rally against an error that could ever be forgiven, but instead created a whipping boy they could stand up there and be superior against.

Cathy. She waved there in that flag. But it was the old Cathy, plump and comfortable, plain and meek, mindless of the crowd. Now she was the last thing he needed—one of them always around to hinder him from being a man by his terms. She'd keep him from that quiet contentment he could have in the garage with his cup of coffee and a ball-peen hammer, someone's deer-smashed fender, and the promise of a Saturday night race that he'd need to re-paint the 2B on his door panels for, then freshen his decals and tune his engine, do it all the best a body-man's means would allow. Just be his own racer, not something he wasn't meant to be—that shame they starve to make little, then prod to compete ferociously and formidably, gone from their consciences so they can feel big and right against it.

For an instant, before he cut any harder into the down-stater, Lucas wondered if those flying checkers would mark not a win, but just more procrastination in learning to live with what events had made of his days, his nights. Maybe this was a chance to race his ass right out of a world where he needed Cathy and checkered flags to prove he was worth something, to finish exactly where he needed to be.

As the three knotted cars righted themselves between a zig and a zag, the crowd pouring down the bleachers, some press-ing sneered faces into the fence and clawing its chain-links, he veered left, freeing his car, separating the field, so he raced not by wile, not by clinging at drivers to slow them, but car to car. He raced by the confines of the old leaky-piston engine Lucas Ogden rebuilt and repaired, his fortune sealed by a tire he'd blown in his desperation.

On its own now, the car slowed, the flat tire sucking it down to the edge of the track. Released from Lucas, the down-stater and College Boy shot away, swinging under the lapped car. Lucas kept on the gas and fought the wheel to the finish, those check-ers flourishing as wildly over him as they just had as College Boy nosed past the down-stater.

Lucas lifted off the accelerator, let go of the wheel, and loos-ened his helmet strap as the flat tire, still holding to the rim, drew him leftward through turn two. One by one, the grind of each cranking engine ebbed out of this glowing bowl of yellow track light, delivering Lucas into the soothing chug of his pistons as he crawled along at a slow, throaty idle. He glanced across the infield to the fence where the white sheet, spray-painted with its blue and red Not 2B, drooped motionless in that calm that fol-lows the fury of these Saturday night races for glory. And think-ing he'd done right by his banner, Lucas cared not anymore to drive so fast that he could tear a sheet to tatters.

NANCY

In John O'Hara's signature novel, *Appointment in Samarra*, the central character, Julian English, is a man of the high society of cocktails and intrigue. Embroiled in great scandal and disgrace, he flees town in a Cadillac. But after an hour on the road, he stops, turns around, and goes back to face his shame.

As Julian returns, he

> *wished he had gone on instead of turning around. To go on until he had spent his money, write a check in Harrisburg, write another in Pittsburgh, until his money was gone; then sell the car, sell it and buy a second-hand Ford, sell his coat, sell his watch, then sell the Ford, then get a job in a lumber camp or something—where he wouldn't last a minute, not a day. . . . You did not really get away from whatever it was he was going back to, and whatever it was, he had to face it. His practical sense told him that the idea of going away, writing checks, selling the car and so on, eventually would catch up to him. He probably would break a law. . . . And so he kept his foot on the accelerator, hurrying back . . .*

Would it have caught up to him? Would he have broken a law?

Just what might come of a man in similar circumstances, whether then or in years before, if he decided to keep going instead of turning back, really decided to run from it all?

What if he found that lumber camp?

≈ ≈ ≈

Spencer W. Elkin, if that was his name, lay now up Shade's Draft in one of three graves dug on the high side of an apple tree, where the spring freshets won't wash him out. He's between another woodhick, whose past, too, is probably colorful but unholy, and the mulatto, Nancy Shade.

Elkin was a dandy the day he come to camp, tailored suit with white pinstripes, a stiff bowler he went right on wearing—even though among the wares for sale in the crew boss's shanty were brimmed hats to keep off the rain. However, he did buy trousers, a Woolrich flannel, and high-heeled logger boots, then hung that suit from a nail in the rafter above his bunk. And underneath, he parked his wing-tipped shoes.

He wasn't all proud. First day out, Elkin admitted to the woods boss that he wouldn't last the season giving his all. But a wild Allegheny hollow was where he needed to be, and he'd swing an axe and swamp branches to his death for a chance to lay low.

So that tuned our ears for his story, and we came to know pieces of it roundabout by what he spoke in the woods. And by his unhealthy fear of the dark, which showed itself before long. When the fever set in, we chinked the gaps.

This we learned: In the 48-hours preceding Elkin showing up at the camp door, his wife had caught him tomcatting, his mistress had dumped him, he'd thrown a drink in the face of a man he owed $5,000, punched out a one-armed brother-in-law (a veteran of Cuba, at that), and taken a brand new Hudson automobile from his father-in-law's dealership. He'd fled town hauling a case of bourbon in the mother-in-law seat—booze meant for his wife's thirtieth birthday party—and half the $5,000.

He'd driven six hours northeastward, and then by chance and fear, landed up with us.

It was dusk of early June. What tree frogs that could find a tree had started burping out their love notes, and moths already tapped at the windows of the feed hall.

Eating was as serious and competitive work in a logging camp as felling was in the woods, and the price of a full stomach was talking. So with not much being said, we clearly heard his fancy wooden heels mount the two steps to the door. But what got our attention, what stopped all fork-fulls of kraut and pork, was that he knocked. You don't need to knock at a lumber camp.

An old-timer lobby hog who kept the bunkhouse and maintained the peace, name of Sholly Giles, was by seniority camp sentry. Even he looked confused. Then, as though he'd put on a black jacket with a tail, he rose from his space closest to the kitchen, walked over, and opened the three-plank door.

There stood Spencer W. Elkin, coat over his arm, hat in hand, as if he'd come to join us in a billiards tournament. You knew just by the cock of his chin and lift of his shoulders that he was given to pinching ready-made cigarettes between two fingers, out in front of him where he'd hold a hand of cards. And that in a closet somewhere, he had many more fine suits. He had about him an air of money and mahogany furniture and that refinement that's musky with favors some women dole out for the prospects that men like him carry in their pockets.

But behind those black eyes, he was scared, almost as much by the wolves he faced as whatever chased him there.

"Where in hell'd you fall from?" said the cook, Dutch. He stood at the kitchen doorway, wiping his hands down his apron.

"Come for a job," Elkin said. "They tell me in that little town on back, there's work."

"On back?" old Sholly Giles said, pinching Elkin's sleeve and yanking him in, though all the flies had already abandoned the pigsty in favor of the fume of kraut. "Sinnemahoning's six miles down hollow."

Elkin nodded. That was the place.

"You walked up the rail line? In them shoes?"

Fifteen woodhicks stretched their necks to look at his feet.

Elkin seemed to have an idea. He reached to his back pocket as if for a bone to throw at this pack of wolves. Or maybe a bottle to calm his nerves—we all got real interested. Then his hand come round with a billfold.

"I could pay for some dinner," he said.

We laughed. If a man could buy grub in the feed hall of a logging camp, he didn't need work in the woods.

⌒

He was from near Philly-delphia. We knew nothing of that part of the state, for it was not a place woodhicks came from, rather a privileged kingdom where the sons of the tier's doctors and newspapermen went to learn to become doctors and newspapermen, and where our girls went to become house servants.

We were working a tract called Barry Hollow, and it had, as we joked, a dark past. Dark as in secret—once home to two escapees. Dark as in black folk, as were those escapees who'd come there to hide over a half-century before. One was Bartholomew Jones, which accounted for the name Barry Hollow and the creek being called Barry Run. He'd squatted near its mouth where the waters spilled into the Sinnemahoning Creek, major feeder to the log-toting West Branch of the Susquehanna. And uphollow, right below the site of our old camp, there still grows among the pine and hemlock stumps a lone apple tree near a ditch from a latrine. The tree stands at the base of a side-hollow called Shade's Draft. The draft, a narrow canyon, bears the name of another squatter, a man of coal-black skin who'd never had a last name, so had come to use his handle for one, thereby calling himself John Shade.

The flanks of that draft were so treacherous we had to suspend ourselves with hemp rope to fell its hemlocks. An eerie place it was, so steep and confined it stayed gloomy midday.

They're long gone, Shade and Jones, shooed out of their shacks after the Civil War, Jones by a farmer and Shade by one of the lumber barons that sliced themselves tracts of the big woods and started the large-scale logging. With no place to go, the pair boarded together in Sinnemahoning, and somehow, despite the spurn of 600 inhabitants—staunch abolitionists or not—each took up with a woman in a shanty at either end of town and fathered children, the mulattos as they were known on the street. The children scattered away years ago to the industrial burgs of the tier where bosses or lovers would have to guess at their dark skin and curls. All except Nancy Shade, who after her mother and father died, stayed on in their shack downstream of town, across from the mouth of Barry Run. Her goats mowed a skinny grass-flat while she sold cheese and milk for the lumber camps and took in loggers' laundry and sewing. Every woodhick said he knew of a man she'd taken in as well—never himself, of course. It wasn't a far stretch to have your pants off there, though, since some of us only owned one set of work clothes.

Spencer Elkin kept up with us in the woods into the heat and bugs of July, snake season, we called it, when it seemed for every kerf cut, a feller had to axe a rattler. But Elkin lasted only by something furiously possessing his body. There seemed two halves of the man, one a leaf of graying flesh withering around a stalk of stooping bones, the other what the Dutch woodhicks called his doppelganger, a demon double that harassed him daylong, itself fearing an even greater evil waiting in that darkness Elkin shunned. It wielded over him a whip, drove him like a slave. Sometimes we'd have to stop Elkin from chopping away at a bole after he'd axed a limb off, frothing at the mouth, trying to bore clear through as if to kill a serpent on the other side.

But as soon as dusk neared, we were sure to see Elkin along a skid trail, wide-eyed, on the lookout for a team pulling a log. Then he'd follow like a little boy to the landing and wait there with the crew for the train ride back to camp. On the way in, standing among the men in the tender, he'd fall asleep. But he clutched his axe, knuckles white, as if to keep his doppelganger from prying it away.

∾

It's a bad sign when a woodhick's too tired for dinner. But before the crew boss could fire Elkin, Dutch got to feeling bad for him. He took him on in the kitchen, told the crew boss that Elkin could give a hand until he strengthened and the weather cooled. After all, we needed all the woods help we could get.

Dutch didn't feel bad enough, though, to let Elkin bunk in the kitchen like cooks and cookees did. Even so, the arrangement made for such bad blood with the cookee that Elkin would have been as well off fighting the woods whippings of his doppelganger.

When the cookee learned Elkin was afraid of the dark, he, of course, passed to him any chores that put him outside before or after daylight. He'd send Elkin to the spring or woodpile without a lantern, and he especially liked having him take out the dirty wash water. See, it was necessary to dump the suds and their soggy bits of pork and cabbage far from camp—not only to keep the stink away from the overhead sleeping quarters, but because it attracted flies and vermin such as mice and shrews. Vermin attracted rattlers.

"Come watch him," the cookee would say, and those of us having an evening smoke in the feed hall would crowd up to either of the windows facing the yard. Elkin stuttered along, balancing the tub of grease-skimmed water out front of his chest.

The glow of a lantern arced into the yard from beside the door, lit for the return of the teamsters in the barn currying and salving their Percherons. On moonless nights, Elkin would inch more hesitantly the closer he got to the edge of the light. Alongside one of the oaks left standing for camp shade, he'd peer out, black there as a bucket of pitch. He'd lean as if at a precipice over un-seeable eternity where nonetheless he might catch a peek. We could all but feel in his rigid, shivering calves a mad hankering to know the shape of something he heard there among the choir of woods whispers: that pattering of leaves by night creatures, the cranking of crickets, the bubbling of Barry Run, altogether the stew of din we took for quiet on still nights. While that sound rubbed numb on us, it was to Spencer Elkin a layer of the unknown, and out of it, he expected at any moment some fiend to come crashing.

"Watch him now," the cookee would say. And Elkin would tip that washbasin and shriek to stave off whatever waited out there, then turn and scamper back to camp, best a sickly man could.

~

The first morning that he didn't go down before breakfast, we made up that one of his eyes swelled shut with a toothache and that he planned to have it pulled in town Saturday. A trip to town was a stretch for him, for he wouldn't have been lured anywhere public for all the fancy women in the commonwealth. In fact, he was upstairs shivering under three horse blankets, lanterns lit—he'd begged the lobby hog to leave them burning till daybreak.

Normally, we'd have sent a sick man out of camp, but he'd offered us a deal. Told us his Hudson Roadster was hid in a mule stable way down off the new state highway toward Williamsport. In its backseat was the case of liquor, the cash stuffed in the upholstery. It'd go to the men who kept him out of hospital and graveyard or anyplace else where his name might breathe into an easterly wind. "Just keep me alive and hidden," he whispered from under the blankets, "and I'll take you there."

By the end of the week, we were taking him to the mulatto.

∽

We had no choice. Three days after Elkin went bedrid, the lobby hog took ill. At breakfast, we tried to explain Sholly's disappearance as a spree, but the cook knew that lobby hogs never played hooky. As we made up better lies, the cook eyed a wet spot on the ceiling. We followed him upstairs where he found a quivering pile of wool, and beneath that, Elkin. He'd sweated out every ounce of water we'd poured down his throat, clear through his blankets to where they draped to the floorboards.

"You gut-damned fools," the cook said. "You'll kill the whole camp. *Get him out.*" He flapped his dishtowel at the stairs.

Then he went to the lobby hog's bunk and pulled back the blankets. "Thunder and lightning," the cook said. Old Sholly Giles was gone, the soul of his eyes shelled out, husks aimed at heaven's gates.

∽

The Barry Run camp was unusual. We'd built it high, near a spring we dug on a flat above the confluence of Shade's Draft and Barry Hollow, for the creek bottom was too narrow that far uphollow to have quarters along the rail grade. Everyone complained about the steep hike from the train when we returned at night.

Any timber from the ridge, we'd skidded to a log slide that snaked from near camp to a landing at the mouth of Shade's Draft. That was the best way to get Elkin to the train.

"Strap him to a plank," the crew boss said when he came to look at Elkin. We'd backed tight to the perimeter of the bunkhouse. He surveyed us. "Idiots," he said, then mumbled he'd fire us. But we knew he would not—he needed to get a hollow-full of timber moved by winter, and crews were hard to gather by then. What did we care anyway? There was money along the state highway. We just needed to keep an eye on Elkin. By then, we even had security—we'd threatened out of him the key to the motorcar magneto. Before he gave in to the influenza, we'd have from him where that Hudson was hid.

∾

On a stump out back, we tied a rope to each end of Elkin's plank, then took him over and fitted him in the v-notch made by the halved logs of the slide.

The crew boss came out and ordered the engineer to dead-head him into town.

"To the mill?" the engineer said, keeping a distance in the camp yard. His fireman stood at his elbow, peering at the bundle of wool, motionless now, quiet.

The crew boss had already started toward his office shanty. He turned back. "Not the mill, you idiot. Get him to the station and off to a hospital."

Of course, he wouldn't want Elkin taken to the mill where word would spread quickest that the influenza had made a summer run in his camp. That was bad for recruiting, like syphilis in the whorehouse.

The cook called from the camp steps. "What about Sholly?"

The crew boss pointed into Shade's Draft. "The ones not taking the train," he said, "bury him." He stood near the tree where Elkin threw the wash water at night, waving away flies. "Coroner wouldn't even know who to send the papers to."

∾

The closest hospital was an hour train ride beyond Sinnema-honing. But we'd made our bargain—Elkin was to be hid. So we bribed the engineer to drop us near the mulatto's.

The slide was steep, near plumb on the final stretch where it spilled into Shade's Draft. From that point, we wildcatted logs—let them shoot and crash into the rough and tumble landing along the rails.

"What-a we do from here?" said a teamster who had hold of a guide rope. We stood at the turnaround spot where the man working the drop would chock the butt of the log and skip out the grabs of the chains the horses used to pull it that far. He'd knock the chock away with a maul, and the log would rasp and roar down the chute. Elkin peeped out from the new blankets we'd tied around him with butcher twine, mummy-like. He stared into a sky where once reared stout hemlocks, the heavens a blue of old denim that day, light and somehow inflated, a high faded sky.

"Ain't got rope enough to ease him from here," a man mumbled under his logger's mustaches. He peered down the slope and shrugged as if he'd turn around and go back for a nap on this strange day off. But everyone started counting how much money fit in their pockets, and moments later, more rope appeared with the stable boy. We got to either side of the slide, took up the line, and eased Elkin down to where the engineer had stoked the Shay. The fireman was busy shoveling coal to make a flat spot where we'd lay Elkin in the tender.

We crowded around him on the coal pile, holding that plank tight. If the influenza didn't kill him before we got to the mulatto's, the dips and shifts of temporary track would rattle the haunts right out of him.

∽

The rail grade reached the valley at the farm of Leonard Hugh. Hugh's steep fields fed our teamsters straw and oats, and his son helped the cook with the butchering of hogs. Their home and barn occupied a knoll beside the mouth of Barry Run, looking over the bigger water.

It was on that knoll that Bartholomew Jones had squatted, the ground he'd broke and planted with potatoes. Several trees in the apple orchard back of Hugh's house, Jones had reared, from seed. But along came Hugh to uproot Jones—he'd acquired the bottom 100 acres of the hollow and the sweeping ridges to each side after his service in the war.

By our day, mostly Hugh's boy farmed the place. He did not admit that a black man had settled it before his family, claimed at the Grange meetings in Sinnemahoning that his father was a pioneer of the valley and that Jones had been a thieving escapee whom the Elder Hugh had let squat there. The math didn't work out.

While we cradled Elkin, we watched that tall, two-story home with its white-painted clapboards and double chimneys. He'd taken again to shivering, kept gasping out that we'd laid him on ice, that he couldn't endure the sledging ache between his heels and withers.

"Old lady Hugh is a midwife," a local fellow said, lifting his chin at the house. "That's half a nurse."

We shook our heads—then he did, too—and looked up at the soot-stained ceiling arch of the Pennsy underpass. Coming out the other side, the engine veered toward the mill, tracing the bank of the Sinnemahoning Creek below the grade of the main line. Across the water, on a silver-green grass-flat, stood the mulatto's shack.

The only dry route to her place was to go clear into town, cross the bridge, and take a mule trail back. So it was a swim in springtime or a wade in summer, which we'd all done—to deliver our clothes or buy goat cheese, of course. Word was the

new state highway, making its way clear to Sinnemahoning from
Williamsport, would cross her place by next summer.

The engineer let us off and continued onward to turn around
at the mill. We waded across, slipping and tottering on the
cobblestone but careful to keep Elkin shoulder-high, out of the
water. We rested on the other side, setting him on a sandbar, and
he grunted to let us know he was alive. That wasn't necessary,
though, with him quaking again, in a fit now like the reared tail
of a rattlesnake.

Nancy's shack was little more than a stable, and not just
because it looked like one. Those billy-goats and nannies made
themselves at home, hoofing creek sand all over her pine-plank
floor, finding shade in summer, stove warmth in winter.

We hauled Elkin up the creek bank and through the saw
grass to her loamy yard. Over a pair of her bearded beasts, she
peered out the door, all white eyes and cinnamon hair, which she
let grow wild as greenbrier.

"Nancy," the local fellow said, "it's boys from up the Barry
camp. We got a man we want you to tend. Needs nursed healthy
with your goat's milk and medicines."

Nancy eyed the trembling bundle we'd set on the ground.
"I ain't a doctor." She pointed toward Sinnemahoning. "Take
whatever that is to town."

"Can't," the local said, then lied: "Doctor says the only
chance is your kinda medicine. Says Elkin here's too bad-off for
a regular doctor, that your place's better than even a hospital.

Nancy laughed. "Don't give me your tales spun in the woods
with whiskey. Get away from here."

She disappeared into the darkness of her shanty, and we
looked down at the frog eyes staring from the bundle of wool.

"Elkin."

He blinked.

"We taken you here to Nancy instead of a hospital. Or worse. You see?"

He grunted a yes.

"So now give us the coordinates on that automobile."

Elkin closed his eyes.

"We'll take you back to the creek," a woodhick in a slouch hat said. "But not to the other side."

Another said, "You'll hope that board stays upright, clean to Williamsport."

A trail of wool wiggled as if a mouse sneaked through, and out came Elkin's hand. He pointed to his lips. They were withered and papery as birch bark. Someone went to the creek and soaked a handkerchief, came back, and wrung it over his face.

"Farm thatta way," Elkin gasped, lifting his finger to point downstream.

"We know that," said several woodhicks, impatient already.

"Barn's round."

Everyone looked at the local fellow. He shrugged.

"What if there's more than one round barn?" said the big one we called Scandinavia.

Elkin just lifted his hand.

"Where's the mule stable from the barn?" said the red-faced smitty.

"Back," Elkin said. "By the creek."

We all drew pictures in our minds, but only Scandinavia thought to ask the farmer's name.

Elkin's eyes shifted back and forth. "German fellow."

                       ◌

She stumbled up the flank of the draft on a Sunday, hitching her dress, soaked through. Weren't a bit of weight to her no more, and her eyes had sunk into her skull. The cinnamon hair was a tangle of knots and burrs like the coat of a feral dog. She

staggered toward the boiling wash kettle back of camp where
the fellows had hooted at her coming up the slope. They quieted
quick though when someone remembered aloud that the crew
boss should not hear from Nancy Shade, seeing God and her
alone knew we hadn't delivered Spencer W. Elkin to a doctor.

As for the crew boss, it wouldn't have done anyway for him
to find a woman in camp, let alone a mulatto woman, let alone
a mulatto woman shivering from the influenza.

Nancy came right up to the ring of stones where we made
our fire for washing, a few men naked, pushing down on themselves from just the sight of a woman. The fellows around the
camp yard not tending the kettle—or not washing that Sunday,
having plans to go to Nancy—came to hear what brought her.

Only one of ours had got the influenza bad—a few others
had sweated it out. That was while we were blowing the sin outta
our pants in Williamsport, so we'd been able to put the sick
one in the hospital there quick. Then we went right back to our
lechery, the richest, best-dressed woodhicks that town and its
ladies ever saw.

Between cat houses and card tables, Elkin's $2,500 had lasted
the lot of us five days. We left his motorcar at that same farm off
the state highway. When we got to camp—it'd been more than a
week by then—the crew boss was almost glad we'd taken leave,
aired the place of the influenza. We knew we'd have our jobs
back, what with new crews hard to come by. Our little holiday
had nearly shut down the operation.

Nancy bowed over, leaning on a stick she carried.

"Doing house calls now?" said the one stirring the kettle.
"For wash, I mean." We all laughed, even as nervous as we were.

"That man's dead in my house," Nancy said. "You gotta
come and get him."

"That man was a drifter," the local fellow said. "We wouldn't
know where to send him."

"Don't matter," she said, stooping lower, wheezing more than talking, "you got to get him and bury him. Anyways, you lie." She coughed, coughed like something tried to crawl out. "You know about his money. That'll bury him. I got no money. And I need some for a doctor." She hacked and spat, and the men closest to her moved away. "He said you could get me his money. I nursed that man. Now give me my due, or you'll have two to bury."

Scandinavia pulled out his jackknife, stepped to the fire, and shaved flakes of lye into the kettle of lousy union suits. "If we knew about any money," he said, "there'd be a Chinaman folding our britches right now. We wouldn't be out here sawing trees a nickel apiece. Now get outta here, you. Stop accusin' us a robbin' a poor dead man." He shrugged, hadn't looked at her. "Maybe you just didn't give him any potions so he wouldn't burdent you."

Nancy swayed against her stick, tried to right herself. She fell back, legs in the air. Our loins weren't so unloaded that we didn't glance about, thinking of turns.

"I'm da-dying," she said, getting herself to sitting, slow like she was just waking up. She coughed, phlegm catching on her chin like one of her goat's beards. "Get that money, back the state highway like he told ya, and help me." She waited a minute to get her breathing right. "Ain't anyone in town that'll help a poor black girl."

She crawled to a pile of bed ticks yet to be washed and rubbed her face in them. There wasn't anything left on her bones to round out her behind like we'd all known it.

Each man looked away to the boiling kettle like it was his turn next to ladle out the suits. So we didn't notice the crew boss watching until he hollered from alongside the smitty's shed.

"What's that?" he said, pointing where Nancy squirmed among the ticks. With her dress old and faded, her skin gone ash gray, the whole mess looked like a sack of snakes.

"Old Nancy's come up," the local fellow called back. "Gone crazy. Wantin' to do our wash there."

The crew boss narrowed his eyes at the heap, Nancy gathering herself to sitting. She raised a hand toward him, tried to speak. But she appeared to keep forgetting where she was, looking at us by the fire for a bearing, eyes floating in the sockets of her skull like doughnut-holes in a mug of coffee.

"Send her on her way," the crew boss yelled. "Now." He pointed at the log slide. "Or you're done. You used up all your second chances here."

❧

If the crew boss hadn't been watching, I suppose we'd have been kinder in how we dragged Nancy on the slide. We aimed her legs-first and pulled her along, dress turning up over her stomach, naked underneath, the dank of fever, of woman. She seemed not to have possession of her limbs anymore, exhausted and out of sorts. And she spoke no sense, just mumbled about her goats. The stable boy slid down the plumb part with her, gathering her limbs as they went. She was so sticky-wet she slowed the pair, almost put them to tumbling.

At the bottom, alongside the tracks, we couldn't get her to sit up.

"She ain't gonna make it," Scandinavia said, looking down the rail grade where the apple tree leaned near the tracks at the side-hollow of Shade's Draft. He shook his head back and forth, and we all knew what he was thinking. "I ain't about to carry her clear to the bottom of the hollow. Then turn around with Elkin just to go back for her."

Everyone nodded.

Scandinavia pointed to the stable boy. "Climb up and get them bed ticks." He looked from face to face. "We'll let her here tonight, have someone keep a watch on account of the bears and wildcats scavenging. If by chance she's alive and over the shivers when the log train comes in the morning, we'll send her down on the locomotive."

"What'll we sleep on tonight?" the stable boy said.

Everyone looked at him, and Scandinavia said, "Now you're the one's gonna dig Elkin's grave." He nodded toward the apple tree. "Long side the lobby hog's."

Scandinavia turned to Nancy, who'd rolled onto her side, balled up, rasping, "ga, ga, ga . . . ," unable to get out even "goat."

"Make it two," Scandinavia said.

THE WAGON WOMAN

The highway courses town like poisoned lifeblood, keeping Arroyo alive but killing it all the while. Still, it flows on, the main event, the primary thing around here. A person would think the highway came first, and the town festered around it, like a gall on a goldenrod stem.

I'd like to say I never judged the wagon woman. But we all did; we all had an opinion of her. And of those kids, of course.

It eventually came down to that—how anyone would presume her blameworthy. But when I had no choice except to think about it, I came to see her differently, as I see the world now in a very scary way. What's scarier, though, is how others go on feeling the same after what happened.

❧

Arroyo is small and tight-knit. But it's become mostly a bedroom community, even if the furniture plant still goes strong. The other factories—the empty tile works and engine shop and lumber mill—all lean decrepitly and hollow-looking, like the old-timers who worked them and spend their afternoons now on porch benches at the Legion Post.

Most working people drive fifteen miles to strip mall shops, medical clinics, or warehouses in Kotsburg, the county seat—"town" as we ironically call it these days. They shop there too, saying they need the better selection at the supercenter and home improvement store.

Like I said, the highway's a lifeline and a shearing blade of death, both at once. It's only a matter of time before we lose our hardware and grocery, the bedroom complete, and the highway just an artery feeding some mutated limb of Kotsburg.

But it does not matter to me anymore if we lose our hardware and grocery, places the wagon woman used to go to.

༄

With so many old folks in town and the highway being what it is, we get mainly two kinds of calls at the ambulance station, or the depot as we call it—cardiacs and car wrecks. The cardiacs come mostly in the morning when we often find them near the toilet, and the wrecks later in the day when people are most in a hurry.

I've always been watchful—nosey, my wife would say—so am good at picking up on these patterns, unlike her, who drives focused and never looks around in church, which I believe is actually more dangerous to the body, though a little safer for the soul. We all fall into routines. And I have seen, out on the highway, how they can collide. Sometimes they strike violently and turn back on themselves, roaring away in waves that break and crash well beyond impact, stomping and scattering everything to debris. I have been part of this.

༄

I came to see that the wagon woman, out most every day, left at a consistent time on Wednesday mornings from her home right there along the highway. She pulled her little girl and baby boy in a rusty wagon with wobbly white wheels. Its makeshift wooden rail, attached to the metal side panels with tomato stakes, kept those kids upright and inside as she trundled along. And since I passed through at different times, having breakfast at home some days, but more and more at the diner, I got to know their Wednesday route. And leaving late a few times, I even learned their destination.

You get to know a lot of routines when you're observant. I'd recognize acquaintances and old classmates going by in their cars, on their way to work in Kotsburg or to drop off kids at school. Elderly in-laws and uncles, too, would pass, headed to the Legion.

That's how I came to know the pattern of my old girlfriend, Pam. And one morning on Main, we cracked ice fifteen years thick by waving, starting our own pattern, and breaking that supposed anonymity of the road.

After she passed that day, taking her kids to the Arroyo Daycare from where she'd turn back and head to her PR job at the Kotsburg Hospital, I tried to recall who waved first.

∽

It was on the Wednesdays I stopped at the Sixty-One Diner that I connected at a consistent place in the wagon woman's routine. I'd sit at my booth in a nook beside the entranceway where I could look out my own picture window at the road. I liked it there where the ceiling fans fed me the homey smells of coffee and fresh pastries, away from the grease and steam at the counter. From there, I saw her closest, out where the place fronted the highway so tightly you couldn't park: flat and round face, thick-rimmed, coaster-wide glasses, butch hair luster-less and sheaved with early gray she didn't color, like maple bark.

Until she went by, there was always an expectant air in the place, the regulars at their swivel stools quieter against the tinny sound of the AM radio announcer tinkling out his newscast, a voice as familiar as a neighbor uncle's. Then there'd be a dead pause while she trudged past the two picture windows, tugging that wagon so old and scarred it must have been hers as a child. And the kids, smiling and looking around like *wee this is fun*, unaware that everyone thought they looked ridiculous, that their mother should be arrested for exposing them to danger like that as she pulled them along the puddle-pocked berm, past the scattered highway houses on the outskirts of town, not safe and secure in car seats.

After the wagon woman passed, Molly the waitress, back behind the u-shaped counter, would flick a glance at the steam-stained mosaic of ceiling tiles and make a tsk, which caught up and down the counter fast and sure as criticism always does about those out of convention. I'd condemn, too, a sad shake of my head and a sigh for the stupidity of some people. Then we'd all agree there ought to be a license, somehow annoyed by that face forever fixed in toothy bliss. It was as if, in the same obliviousness that she went around as a pedestrian despite a cargo of children, the wagon woman actually thought the day was some sunny affair.

I knew that Wednesday routine as well by how it differed from the rest of the week. On calls other mornings, I'd catch her later, heading out the highway or returning along the sidewalk on Main, white grocery bags and jugs of milk piled around the little ones, or maybe a broom from the hardware poking out. But still, that insensible, claw-tooth grin, the wagon woman towing her pathetic kids contently as a sled dog.

⌒

The Sixty-One Diner is on the outskirts of town, out the highway before the depot. Pam lives on a hillside of expensive homes on that side of town, while her daycare is near me on Main. That's how I'd catch her passing some mornings. And since she had always been the kind of girl to look around, she must have seen my car outside the diner on days I'd left early.

The first time she came, it was yet quiet—a Wednesday, and the wagon woman hadn't gone by. The only noise above the radio and the subdued murmur was the chatter of coffee cups and saucers Molly stacked in a bus tub along the counter. I'd just stepped back to my booth from having a cigarette outside—yes, like so many E.M.T.s, I smoke in the face of that reality we encounter every day, wheeling away lung patients who gasp for breath, or ones who'd gasped their last. We're typically drinkers, too, though most of us draw the line at putting a car on the highway.

I dated a lot over the years, and I can tell you there is always some main feature a man remembers about an old girlfriend, and it's the first thing that comes to mind whenever he encounters her. Usually, it's very personal, private. While it may not be sexual, it's always bodily—the way her hips move, or a smell or heat she seems to breathe out, sometimes even a region of her that tunes a homing sense. I know it is very deep-rooted, maybe primitive, for I've felt this stir right near the part of my brain that calls out hunger and thirst, that tastes.

When Pam stepped through the door that July morning, every neck at the counter swiveled. I don't know if she intended to turn at that moment to my booth or if the mass stare of retirees and of businesspeople on their way to Kotsburg sent her to my nook as a sanctuary. But she came, the steam of my fresh cup jittering in a waft of perfume as she shrugged off her purse strap and swooped onto the vinyl bench opposite me. She looked across the blue ice of age, that condensed time between old friends that is so solid and passable you can skip right over all that happened between. In that instant, my mind homed on the landmark of all my memories of Pam, and I knew I should leave. But I did not.

Now this goes back to high school and the two years afterward when I attended with Pam—and then quit—the state college branch-campus in Kotsburg: whenever I touched her ribs just below the side of her breast, whether we danced in a gymnasium or petted in the little Ford pickup I drove those days, there was a sensation at the palm of my hand that I cannot describe as anything but glitter, which sifted up my arm and across my shoulders, then poured down my spine and fizzed in my loins. And I could see there in the diner, up close to her silky beige blouse, that although fifteen years and the wear of three childbirths had rounded and wilted—some—a once rigid figure, that spot on her ribs, where my thumb could nest right beneath the cushion of her breast, remained unchanged.

Behind the hospitable, closed-mouth smile I gave Pam, my mind raced to measure all the personal gains and losses of age that occur to a person in those situations: waistline, hairline, last bout of adult acne. But Pam looked nowhere but into my eyes, and that made me feel as if I'd climbed back into my eighteen-year-old self.

"Josh," she said. "Nice to finally see you someplace we're not buzzing past each other. Like down at the carnival or out on the highway."

The murmur around the counter had risen slightly, even though it was early Wednesday. The ringing of cups and saucers had ceased because, I realized, Molly stood beside us, tablet in hand. "Slumming, Pam?" She drummed her pen against her pad.

With a big smile and a jingle of bracelets, Pam put her hand to her mouth and laughed, turning the insult into a friendly joke. "Molly, right? I thought you were over at the Quick Scissors?"

And it was like we were all eighteen again, Molly plain and plump and resentful of Pam the cheerleader type, and Pam, holding reign over both of us. Either unconsciously or self-consciously, Molly padded a spray of her big red hair and asked Pam in a flat voice what she'd like.

"Do you have herb tea?" Pam said.

Molly rolled her eyes out the window and back. "Define a herb, and I'll see what I can brew up."

Pam launched that grin of perfect teeth and said any tea would be fine.

Then while she and I went through the routine of job and family, me all the while wondering what the hell she was doing there, I was able to assemble from the old and the new, the Pam she'd become. I'd like to say that had I known she, like so many people who eventually get into trouble, was ignorant of the combination of old and new and wanted some sanctuary from the present in the past, I'd have lied that I had to rush to work. But I know how lukewarm I'd become to myself at that point in my life, and I'd have been willing to ignore any reality even if I'd realized then Pam's momentum. And I suppose somewhere out on that highway, both of us had already glimpsed the sea of time that freezes between old friends and lovers, and while she was trying on a pair of skates, kidding all the while that she'd only turn a few teasing laps, I had already lit a warming fire on the other shore.

୬

Despite Pam giving rise to all the discussion along the counter, the Wednesday pause happened, heads turning toward the luster of morning haze framed by the picture windows. Pam twisted her neck to see the wagon woman pulling her kids steady and determined as a tugboat, same silly, satisfied nonchalance.

When the wagon woman had passed, Molly sighed, then let out her tsk as if she tossed peanuts to a squirrel. And that released the place, the patrons around the counter speaking louder, freer.

"Can you believe she takes those kids around like that?" Pam said, joining our club of wagon woman critics. "I've even seen her haul them under blankets in winter—snow on the ground, ice on the highway." As she shook her head, the jewels that studded her earrings brightened on and off. She closed her eyes. "Those poor kids."

A tractor-trailer roared by, rattling the glass against its frame. "She's out most every day," I said. "But Wednesdays, it's always the same time, same route."

"Where does she go?"

"Storybook hour at the library."

Pam shot a finger into the air. "That's right. Daycare takes my kids there sometimes, and Missy's mentioned seeing her." Then she laughed, but only for a second, and I'll never forget the wistfulness I caught as she looked to the ceiling.

"Sometimes," I said, nodding at the window, "I see her go by, and I almost envy her."

Pam tilted her head softly, like the seat of a swing in a breath of wind, and she recovered a pinch of a smile. "You always were sensitive, Josh."

I should have heeded the warning flag in the way she whispered those words. It didn't quite fit the flow of the conversation, a clear indication of where her mind had gone. A familiarity in her voice, if not intimacy, told me she was skating close to my edge, had closed all those years and the concerns of life in a single dash.

Molly set the teacup beside Pam's thousand-dollar hand of golden rings and bracelets, where Pam and I both looked now. The swishing of cars racing off to Kotsburg—that highway noise we learn not to hear except in awkward silence—reared and fell like the gasps of an old smoker's lungs.

"Josh," Pam said, her voice half-out of its whisper, a weary tone of confession in it. "I'm always in a hurry—it's the one thing I just can't stand."

So often, I see now, we escape into more of what we want to lose.

❧

Because everyone liked calling her the wagon woman, we never bothered to learn her name. I didn't even realize until afterward that I knew her husband. Of course, we all wondered about him, or I should say we shook our heads at a man letting his wife walk the road, not buying a second car. Word was they didn't even have cable TV. And it seemed a little odd, at least in these times, for a woman to have nothing to do all day but haul her kids to the store or the pool or storybook hour.

Her husband had been a year behind me at school until he left ninth grade for the county vo-tech—a squeaky-voiced kid with an RD address. He didn't look his age, and telling by the sheen of his home-cut hair, did not often bathe. After graduation, he took work at the furniture factory running a lathe. I've learned that he's considered a master craftsman there.

But the wagon woman, even though they tell me she was in his grade, had one of those faces that passed in the halls without me ever seeing it.

Pam, on the other hand, had a face everyone noticed. So there was no way of drinking our coffee and tea anonymously in the diner. For a month or so, I was naïve enough to think the patrons passed us off as old friends with crossing routines, harmless banter.

Even a man in denial can't forever ignore the ripple effect of his routine. Eventually, I tuned to the diner crowd's hushing awareness of what had budded in that front booth. Voices had become softer beneath the tinny radio broadcast and the drone of the hood fan—Wednesdays or not.

The telling quiet of the diner patrons made me confront that I had become consumed by the idea that Pam had been drawn back, interested in my tales and observations of ambulance runs, in my opinions of the world. She'd turned from a life where she'd gained all anyone could ask for. And to think she was someone I'd grown away from years ago. But then, I wondered, had I really?

Through all our movements toward it, we never came out and expressed our willingness for the affair. I suspect most people don't.

∾

The depot is half a mile beyond the diner. With four bays and a complete living area to kill time between calls, it's as nice a facility as you'd find even in Kotsburg, thanks to the generosity of the donor businesses we had in town when it was built thirty years ago. Nowadays, our only big supporter is the furniture factory, so the administrator, Sharon, one other E.M.T., and I are the only paid employees. To keep operating, we rely on volunteers. But with them harder to come by, we cover well beyond working hours. I'm often called out at night, especially for 2 AM alcohol crashes, my wife never complaining.

All that extra time we donate gives us the freedom to be away occasionally during scheduled hours—just so we're close by and have our mobile radios. That's how I stretched our almost daily diner visits without too much trouble, Pam racing off to work later and later. Finally, caught between my embarrassment in front of the diners and the obsessive mind-itch I couldn't cure over this woman who'd come of the girl I'd known, I reached out with the invitation.

"Why don't we meet sometime," I said and took a sip of coffee. "When we aren't so rushed."

That was it, and it felt as hokey as the juncture in a movie where the camera closes in as the mister reaches out to somebody's missus, lifts her onto the deck of his sailboat, or guides her to a corner of his studio. I reached for her fingers to help her off that ice of the years and onto the firm ground of the present. And her saying possibly yes, by not saying no, uncorked into my spine that tingling fizz I'd felt when I touched her side, and it crescendoed all through me like the score to those cheating scenes.

But she kept the charade going, closing her eyes and pursing her lips as if it pained her, as if I'd wrinkled the delicate prettiness of our flirtations. Finally, she voiced her answer quick and casual, no hint of the hyper-yelps my heart made like the fast siren of the ambulance hurrying to a bad call.

"I'm thinking a drive," she said, reaching across the back of her neck and brushing her hair from her collar. "It'd be nice to get away to no place particular."

Get away, I think now. As if we left anywhere on the highway.

$$\sim$$

We imagine we're anonymous and free out there. Reckless nobodies, faceless and unaccountable, rid of whomever we've become.

Our last drive—that's what we called them, as though that's all we did—was in early November. We had a simple routine. I'd tell my wife, Hannah, that I was on back-up and a call had come over the radio. Pam used the lie of a craft club in Kotsburg. I'd park at the depot, walk to the laundromat next door, and wait out back.

She was late, so I leaned against the cinder block wall as it hummed with spin cycles, and I sucked a cigarette, hardly giving myself time to exhale between draws. With the excitement brewing below my gut, I reminisced about an old and true November scent that broke through the exhaust of phony floral fabric softener.

With her using a different lie—spotting deer—I'd pick up Pam on similar nippy November nights. She had lived on a street of skinny plank houses at the rear of the furniture factory, homes that flooded every spring when the usually muddy trough of Arroyo Run filled and spilled over its banks between the houses and the factory. Pam's family might have afforded a better part of town—a sole breadwinner could do all right at the furniture factory in the 90s. Except there were seven children, the youngest brother autistic.

She never let me return her home late. "My parents are irritable enough," she'd say. She'd mention, too, nearly every time we were together, that she did not want her children to grow up in a struggling household. "You don't know," she once said, "what being tired can make a parent do."

We'd head out of town, turn onto some back road and find a plot of standing field corn. I'd park my little pickup among the rows and crack my window to the air I'd spiced and sweetened plowing canes with the front bumper. And we'd do exactly what we were about to do this night, so many years later.

I decided behind the laundromat that this time when I put my palm to that spot on her ribs, I'd hold it there long enough for the remnant of the old me, which had been trying to break from the rest, to sift into her. I'd let it sink to where it reached her core, which was just the old Pam, the girl I'd never wanted to leave me but did when I quit college. The old Pam I knew I'd been reaching back for, the one she'd wanted the old Josh to find. For in her new world, a hard veneer had scabbed over the raw, throbbing life she once felt.

☙

When I opened the door of her big SUV—a maroon motel on wheels—and stepped onto the running board, I saw by her loose shoulders and limp jaw—usually locked rigid with thrill at this time—that things had gone where I knew they would. Either guilt was finally breaking her or her husband, Neil, was on to us.

We rode silently, me ducking until we passed the glowing overheads of the used car dealership. One night we were so bold—or so impatient or impassioned—that we parked along the back row. The only steamed windows and trembling chassis on the lot.

When we were far enough past that we could see the lighted sky over Kotsburg, she let herself wretch out the sob she'd been holding. "If it weren't for the kids," she said, "we could keep driving and driving. Not keep turning back just to start off again like a couple bandits."

"Your kids?" I hoped she didn't mean it the way it sounded.

She looked at me long enough to veer into the other lane, her face ghoulish green in the glow of dash lights. "Who the hell's kids would I mean?" She lurched the vehicle back. "I'm not saying I blame them. It's just a fact I'm stating. I thought it would tell you how I feel about us."

Pam touched her eyelid so a tear trickled down her finger instead of her mascara. "You don't have kids," she said. "You've got no idea how hard it is to get to your job, to just start your day when you have to feed them and get one to school, then two to daycare. How many times did I have to come back to Arroyo when a kid had a fever or threw up? And of course, Neil's never any help." She rolled her eyes, then reached in front of my face with a slightly parted thumb and forefinger. "I've come this close to losing my job." She snatched her hand away. "Then, every day after work, I race home to taxi off to gymnastics, cub scouts. Last night it was a frigging roller-skating party that four kids showed up for. Then cart them back home and feed three little kids and one big one. Mommy this, Pam that. You just want to get away, Josh." She looked from the road, brows raised. "Can't we somehow? For a while?"

At the sign for the Kotsburg Landfill, I pointed out the tar-and-chip road to turn onto. I believed her—that she did not blame her kids. She probably thought of her weariness as Neil's fault, which allowed me to be perversely turned on by her desperation, by her dependence on me. And though I did feel guilty that I'd led her to speak of her children as she had, I couldn't help taking pleasure having so much effect on the worldly, wealthy Pam she'd become.

To be fair, sympathetic, I tried to picture her kids but could not from the few times I'd seen them. Instead, the child faces I knew best came to me, bobbing like two goslings above the wooden rail of their wagon, little hands holding on to keep upright. And like their mother, that cluelessly giddy contentment in their grins.

"Is something else wrong?" I said. I looked out my window into the bright night, out over the blanket of wilted goldenrod that had overtaken the rolling fields, my eye drawn to a fold where moonlight swam in an old cattle pond.

"Finally," she said, "my eyes are opened to how much of an ass Neil is."

As much as I tried not to, I doubted he earned that. So I used his reputation at the furniture factory to convince myself he was the same at home as he was as superintendent. Most workers considered him a royal asshole, despite the consensus that his tyrant-like management style kept the place going, hence our town. And he'd given a lot of people second chances, even time away to sober up.

"Turn there," I said when the headlights showed a rotting mailbox post.

"That place again? It gives me the creeps," Pam said.

I touched her hand on the wheel. "I can't wait any longer." And she turned onto the weed-grown drive of the weathered-plank farmhouse, its windows, most of the glass broken, framing tattered curtains which in the moonlight looked lamp-lit, though lifeless and weatherworn like the paper scattered along the road by passing garbage trucks.

"I wish there were still fields with corn to drive into," she said.

She parked in the same spot she had the last few times, back among the gnarled limbs of apple trees, facing the caved kitchen roof. The barn loomed behind us. The shadow it sliced out of the moonlight gave the secure feel of a blanket but in an odd, primitive way. It was like being awash in that deep, extra sense of warning, or survival maybe, that's overcome me during storms in the dark of night. A narcotic boils out from beneath emotion, where something left in us of cave dwellers, or beyond, can sense danger. Instead of alarm, it soothes my body trance-like. Thunder cracks close by, and my heart—opposite of what you'd think—slows, my mind becomes tranquil, numb. This must be how animals mimic death in the most perilous of moments. If so, we are in error crediting them with great courage.

⌒

Headlights out, in the liquid green glow of the clock, she reclined her seat and reached across the console for my hand. "It came out wrong, Josh, about the kids. I love them beyond all—they're why Neil and I work so hard."

I did not speak, wanting her to stop, knowing the more we talked, the more we'd corrupt things. Keeping our time physical made it feel natural and kept the new Pam and Josh, or the combination of old and new, out of it. I pulled her toward me, put her head on my shoulder.

But she went on. "This is the only peace I have." She closed her eyes. "You feel like my chance to pick back up from a slow pace. To walk through life, not run-run-run." She looked up at me. "How do we bring back the old days in the new?"

That was the first either of us admitted the question we tried to answer. And once she said it, I knew that even if we did revive the old Pam and Josh without destroying the worlds we'd created giving them up, our situation would still eventually define itself.

Since that night, I've learned that I'm strong-minded but weak-willed and even weaker in the flesh. I think Pam is strong-willed but weak-minded, and in light of what happened, that makes her less guilty than I am.

I laid aside any noble sacrifices that might nip fate. I kissed her hard. We pressed until my teeth hurt. And as aggressively as I channeled all my energy and ecstasy to my lips, I ever so lightly put my palm to Pam's ribs, my thumb tucked between her breast and the underwire of her bra. I held it there, and she spilled into me. She filled me until there was no room for anything but what our bodies wanted, no room even for guilt.

⁓

There's a thing about lovemaking that, for most men, is very different from what it is for women. We don't often talk about it, except to someone we have a long history with, our wives perhaps, if we finally shed that emotional armor we wear to bed. Maybe part of my infatuation with Pam was that she had yet to be disenchanted in this thing.

Our peak is absolute, with a drop of appetite so steep we wonder ourselves at the genuineness of the affections that led us there. All our desire—whether that stuff of emotion is chemicals or hormones or love itself or whatever—surges out of us, and in the emptiness in which we lie panting, we come face to face with the ultimate selfishness of our gestures. And often, fear or guilt flood the void. When a man is in the ice of that reality, he finds it very hard to look a knowing woman in the eye.

Warmed by the heat of Pam's slowly expiring desire, I let myself escape into the numbness of sleep there on the reclined seat. Eventually, she slept, too. When I awoke, we were out of the shadow of the barn, the moon glaring through the windshield, the liquid numbers of the clock slapping my consciousness with the bare reality that it was no longer Tuesday. As I shook Pam, shouted her name, and cursed, the green numbers changed to 12:59.

∾

At the courthouse, it all came together why the defense agreed to the preliminary hearing, and I understood that I was a big part of the decision.

Everyone in Arroyo had become an amateur lawyer, and they'd predicted the defense would waive, as is typical. But Pam's attorney risked the hearing, and so risked the D.A. knowing her case if it went to trial, risked letting out any embarrassing information from the scene. All on the confidence that the chief witness, especially the chief witness, would not incriminate that well-to-do woman, the educated wife of the furniture factory superintendent. And so there could be no probable cause to send that mother of three to trial, to prison.

Court convened, and as I leaned on the counter in the magistrate's lobby waiting to be called, I watched two secretaries snort and laugh at the carousel of names they typed into computers from piles of summaries. Through the frosted door of the courtroom came bits of testimony from the investigating officer, the same legal jargon I've heard when subpoenaed to other hearings as a first responder—times and measurements and notes of interviews.

Then I was called.

Though the heavy arm of courthouse law should be orderly and sober, the quarters of our magistrate's hearings is a chaotic, cramped vault of sneers and tears, of lawyers alternately whispering and hollering, and at any given time someone throwing up hands and huffing, whether it be the magistrate or a witness or defendant.

Three cars wouldn't fit in the room, which holds even filing cabinets in the corners and Kinkade landscapes on the walls—nothing like the posh mahogany and marble courtroom upstairs. But it's nonetheless haughty with its high ceiling and arched windows. And over the murmur and the constant shuffling of papers, the room itself grumbles as if bloated with all the misery and accusation it's ingested: old wooden chairs creak with every shift of their occupants; any movement of foot is a drumbeat against the floor planks; the ceiling fan chop-chop-chops on high.

And there was plenty of new misery that day in May.

Two small tables stood at the center of the room, a strip of printout hanging from each: PROSECUTION on one, DEFENSE on the other. A powwow of chairs surrounded either table, with others backed against the walls. In the far corner sat Pam's husband, Neil, looking mean as he might be giving hell at the factory, their boy and two little girls dressed as if it were Easter. Pam's father and mother were there too, his respirator ticking, tubes in his nose, and she, heavyset and in polyester, sniveling into a ball of tissue. I did not look at Pam as I entered, though I could not help her lawyer drawing my eye.

Near the prosecution table—well armed with the young, early-thirties D.A., the even younger assistant D.A., and a legal secretary—sat one man, and in him, too, was misery, but not the kind that can bellow and complain. Rather that which metastasizes into the mind, then rots the body, inside and out. I recalled the boy I knew in school, for he'd somehow regressed, as an old person can look again like his baby pictures.

He watched me as I took the stand, but dead-eyed, the way a road-killed deer looks out at the highway that destroyed it. I took my oath and then the seat in the cubby by the judge, all the resolve to hold my nerve gone in sight of that lifeless, slushy stare of universal blame.

"Tell us, Mr. McNulty," the young D.A. said to me, even while his assistant whispered in his ear and the judge answered some question the defense attorney had asked as I came in, "how you first responded to the call to an accident scene on route sixty-one the morning of November third, last year."

I cleared my throat and waited while the D.A. shared with his entourage a tin of breath mints. "I was at the Sixty-One Diner," I said, "having coffee. Our tone sounded off on my radio—there are certain ones for every ambulance service. I was—" I shrugged, looked away at the court reporter who froze mid-motion, hands held at her machine as she peered over reading glasses—"on duty by then."

The D.A. interrupted, not even looking up from his notes. "Please explain how you could have been on duty if you weren't at the ambulance station."

"I was running a little late that morning, and we're okay to be outside the depot, so long as we're nearby and can respond. We need that policy so we can use volunteers off-hours."

Actually, I'd already stayed in my booth even later than the days Pam came. I sipped coffee as fast as cars buzzed by the window. And for the first time, I had not regarded those ridiculous, cheery faces of the wagon woman's children on their way to storybook hour, so focused was I watching for Pam's SUV. My brain still echoed the names she'd called me the night before when she dropped me off along the highway in front of the depot, blaming me for making her late. Sitting there, hoping she'd come so we could erase all that, I was already reasoning beyond reason, against my little voice of sense, that maybe it did not have to end, that we could still avoid ruining lives. Then my phone buzzed. When I answered, she'd hung up, and she did not pick up when I tried back.

While the D.A. flipped through his notes, Pam's attorney did something that caught my attention. She's a well-known Kotsburg defender, fifty and pretty, a face we all know by her billboard sign before town where the highway turns four-lane, something celebrity-like about her in person. If you can smirk with the eyes, she did it in the flick of a glance at Pam, and in that, I understood why she was so confident that I would not speak an incriminating word about Pam—she'd found out about us. But I was just as confident that Pam had not told her and that the lawyer, sharp by all accounts, had done her homework on me, probably snooped around the diner. How could she be so sure, though, given what happened, that I would not let it spill?

"So why did you go directly to the scene?" the D.A. said. "Weren't you to ride the ambulance?"

"From where I was," I said, "I could get there quicker." I swallowed, then wiped where sweat beaded at my hairline. "The incident was right up the road, toward town, and the depot is the other way." My voice began to break, and I paused, trying to steady it. The judge turned and watched me. "So," I said, "I radioed that I'd go straight to the scene."

The D.A. waited for the judge to look his way, then kept his eyes on him as he asked me his next question. "What did you know about the incident before you arrived?"

"Nothing," I said so quickly that it seemed defensive even to me. "Auto-pedestrian. Trauma. That's it. I knew nothing more about the patients."

At his next question, I tried to relax, reminding myself that this young D.A., unlike the defense, knew nothing of Pam and me, not even the Pam and Josh of old—he'd never have called me as a witness had he known, had he any suspicion I might break and lie. "Mr. McNulty," he said, "please go through the incident from the moment you arrived until other responders joined you. Relate any discussion you had with Pamela Park."

He's after only the facts of the first witness to speak to her, I told myself. At least as he thinks they are. Calm down. It's not like he's going to try to show your testimony as tainted.

The D.A. looked to the stenographer. "I'd like to point out that Mr. McNulty is not an expert witness."

I uncapped my bottle of water and went to sip. Mindless suddenly of my mouth, I splashed my chin. As I wiped it, feeling my hand shake, I closed my eyelids and forced myself to see me racing up Sixty-one to where traffic had stopped. I squeezed my eyes, opened them, and began recounting in a general sketch. I started from where I ran toward the farther of two circles of people at the edge of the oncoming lane, some on knees, others peering over them and waving for my help. Of course, I did not give it in all this detail, which in my mind plays clear as a movie reel.

"Don't touch the patient," I said as I approached, identifying myself as an E.M.T.

I was in call mode, ready to assess, determine what steps to take. I scanned the scene and saw we were beneath the trestle on the curve. The berm across the road, on the way into town, tightens there, forcing any pedestrian to the side we were on.

I shouldered into the circle. "How many injured?"

Because highway incidents often involve multiple injuries, they can require triage—sorting and prioritizing. Treatable patients with severe bleeding or shock receive immediate attention; lesser injuries and imminent death take last priority. However, if there are too few responders in the worst situations, we're faced with choosing among the treatable cases. Triage becomes the icy war term it originally was.

Even though you often know the patient in a small town, you detach into a professional and disassociate the person you know from the body you attend. But when I looked down and saw the wagon woman, torso twisted like a wrung dishrag, eyelids and lips quivering with the effort of words while she drowned in the lifeblood that frothed in her lungs and out her mouth, all the superior snickering I'd let myself take part in turned on me, soured my gut like a flood of castor oil.

She made a word. But not by voice, rather by the will of gurgling into her blood. *"Aye-ees."* I knew immediately she said babies and that her eyes flickered because she tried to see them and not these road vultures. I turned with the pretext of determining triage, but in truth, by the shame her agony enflamed in me and which would, in a moment, sear like a mine fire into the nooks of my brain, into the periphery of everything I'd ever see again.

I pushed my way out of the crowd, hearing the siren of the approaching ambulance as I radioed for a helicopter, knowing it would arrive too late for what I'd seen so far. *"Wagon,"* I cried. *"Waaa-gon."*

And the other circle, a blood trail-away, by the guardrail, opened for me to enter. When I lowered onto my knee, tightening with rage for our capacity to kill children by blunt force trauma, I was struck, through all of it, with how beautiful she was. The soft cheeks—round, puffed yet from her infancy, from her mother's nurturing. The luster of sunlight on the creamy nub of her nose. The curls, the tumbling teddy bears in the fabric of her coat. And of all things, inches from her hand, a children's board book, scraped and dimpled by pavement, opened to the picture of a sad piglet . . . *and this little piggy had none*: no breath, no pulse, no redemption for selfishness.

Again, I pushed people away, begging that someone tell me where the wagon was. They just looked at me, and as I turned circles scanning each side of the highway and peering between the shrubs of homes beside the trestle, I caught trickled blood glistening over the trail of road grease. And then I lost my breath with the impossibility of what I saw. I'd run past Pam's SUV among the bystander's parked cars, not seen it turned off the road with its front bumper buried in a culvert.

The ambulance and fire trucks were arriving, sirens silencing. And as clearly as I still experience the feeling of hallucination that was about to set in, I remember every pock and pebble along the white line of the highway, that annually refreshed paint that faded faster each year as more cars sped off to Kotsburg. As I sprinted along that line, its tar-filled, varicose cracks came to me as the distended veins of some serpent monster we'd borne, a monster raging, spilling venom across the countryside.

⌒

Now the highway comes to me with a smell. I had a friend once—back when I enjoyed such relationships—who could not eat meat after he'd found his grandfather several days dead in a hot upstairs bedroom. The associations I make with the highway are like that—they churn my stomach. I have not been able to look at the road since—I slant my focus over it even as I drive.

Pam sat in the vehicle, windows up, doors locked. And I could hear over the idle of her engine, of all things, the heater blowing. I pounded the glass, still screaming for the wagon. But she made no movement, the long pendants of her earrings still as the morning air.

I've seen enough shock to know that her vision was blank behind the wide eyes, her mind stalled. I went to start away, trace the roadside along the course of carnage, when I saw, extending from beneath the fender where the front of it was planted in the weedy bank of the culvert, a square black handle. I dropped and peered through the wheel well. The wagon part showing was mangled and crushed like a tin can, the vehicle's axel mired in the ditch. And what I thought was a motor mount coated in transmission fluid came to me as a bloody little shoeless foot. Then I was up and beating Pam's window with both fists.

All this I told the court only in summary, adding no detail, none of my impressions, as if I filled out a call report.

"I yelled," I said to the courtroom, rubbing my sweaty palms against my knees, "to put it in four-wheel drive. To back up."

I admitted this, not mentioning I should have known better. It was time to let the firefighters take over with their jacks and cutters. But my personal life and its poor judgment had broken into my call-mode command of myself.

She sat stiff as a highway pole.

Pounding, I purpled my hands before taking from my pocket a window punch and shattering the glass. In a motion, I reached in, opened the door, and unlatched her seatbelt.

"I'm sorry," Pam said as I pulled her out by her blouse. She let out a sob and reached for me to hold her. I pushed her away, and she said, "I wasn't watching the road." Then she wrapped her arms around herself, and in a child's voice, said something I will never come to terms with. "I've ruined them."

Ruined them. As if she'd soiled rag dolls.

But I did not tell the courtroom this, even when the young D.A. held up his hand in a halting gesture. "Did she say anything? Anything before the firefighters showed?"

I shook my head, closed my eyes, and lied, as much for Pam as for weak-willed me. "She said she had no idea what happened. That the curve was blind."

While the D.A. attempted to recover the composure he lost to the point of asking, "Are you sure?" and as Pam's attorney stopped trying to contain her gloating smirk, I just asked if they wanted me to go through the rest. The D.A. could say only no.

But *I* go through the rest, half of me dragging the other in perverse penance. Gripped by shame for my part and for then lying, my only satisfaction is to flail myself with the very horror I want to escape.

After the firefighters jacked and cribbed the SUV, we crawled underneath. The stench of mud and baby flesh and blood that had seared against the hot engine put me to retching, and I choked back vomit as I reached over the wagon metal Pam had rammed between axel and frame.

All because, I realized later, she'd been speeding after dropping off her children late to daycare, rushing to work, and dial-
ing her cellphone. For me.

Even the D.A. assumed Pam made her call after the incident,
though it remained mysterious why she dialed directly to an old-
friend E.M.T., not 911, then hung up. Except to Pam's attorney,
of course, and me. Pam dialed as she took that blind bend, veering into the wider berm on her side, hitting face-first the wagon
woman and her children. The incident, which I will never call
an accident the way her hot-shot Kotsburg attorney did, was not
a case of Pam losing control of her SUV in a glare of sunshine.

But the magistrate had been frowning at his notes. And before
giving me to the defense, he had the stenographer compare from
the policeman's testimony the time on Pam's cellphone record to
the time of the first call to 911, made by a man who'd dialed just
after he'd swerved to avoid the wagon woman and caught, out
ahead, Pam's vehicle going off the road.

With the same grave stare of her billboard picture, Pam's
attorney watched the magistrate mull the call times, his eyes on
the gavel. Meanwhile, the D.A., still bewildered, seemed not
to pick up on any irregularity. Then the magistrate locked eyes
with Pam's attorney. Very deliberately, Pam's attorney turned to
Pam where she sat wilted, the color washed out of her like the
rain-blanched sprays of November goldenrod when they own
the fields outside Arroyo.

The attorney spoke softly, words not so cunning as bold,
for I would never have bet on anyone getting away with such a
hint. But that attorney knows people, knows how easily they are
scared, right down to magistrates. After all, she was the smart-
est one in the room, betting the house on me lying. And the
flustered D.A. let her go, never objected. "All that remains in
our hands," Pam's attorney said, "is to lessen, wherever we can,

the pain of the after, restore some hope for the new." Then she looked at Pam's children, and there was no question she was telling that magistrate where she'd go if this made it to trial, how unlikely it was that anyone would prosecute Pam for vehicular manslaughter with those kids' panicked faces in the courtroom.

∽

A corrupted nursery rhyme chanted in my head over the gnawing of the firefighter's hydraulic tools. Since then, it has not ceased, rapping against the walls of my mind like a pebble in a wheel.

This little piggy lay quivering in the road. This little piggy lay pummeled on the berm. And this *little piggy . . .*

As does a snapshot of that little square foot that had never taken a step, unsullied except for its bathing of blood. I remember how, probing near the foot, I hoped to find some pulse of life until I touched only the smashed flesh of what had been a ridiculously innocent and blissful human being. A baby I'd seen almost every day but had never given much thought, whose blood would later be hosed into a highway drainage ditch after the firefighters extricated his body from the undercarriage they were cutting loose from Pam's SUV.

When they stopped, and we pulled and pried at the wagon, all the world went a-flicker, my heart drumming out a background beat to the frames of a stuttering movie reel. Every odd detail, from dripping blood to ticking engine metal, from the stink of burnt human waste to the spontaneous retraction of my hand from disemboweled parts of that little boy, enlarged and froze and stung, stamping impressions that every night rain across eyelids backlit by the television picture that keeps me company in our living room. Only daybreak delivers me from stifling panic into my one relief, which is merely the calmness of despair.

Between frames, I see how a downpour of that horror leached a man to a skeleton of agony—once a father and husband, now a walking purgatory stalled between life and death.

So which of the innocent do we grieve more, which of them serves the most shame on the guilty—the lives lost, or the ones ruined? My prayer is that there is an answer and that we mourn properly. I saw in that man that we must choose.

❧

I suppose when Pam had gotten home late after dropping me off that night, she fought with Neil, who realized the truth, as even a fool would, and that she reaffirmed her disgust for him as she fell further into that fantasy of running off. Then probably came a long night of remembering her anger with me, and next morning, Pam, just as queasy and torn as I was while I sat in the diner, dawdled herself too late for a breakfast tryst. After she'd finally rushed the kids to daycare, she called, thinking we could erase it all.

Called. Caught, confused, tired. What would it take for her to give up believing she could race away and reconcile her fantasy for the old with the reality of the present?

The scene, the police reports, made it clear that after she'd veered off the road and done it, she'd panicked and gassed with the same impulse that quashed Pam's instincts every time reality scared her, exiting as she had when I was a college dropout and she had kidded herself that we'd ever stop desiring what we'd had. So I am well aware that I, too, pressed on that accelerator. As guilty of not ending the affair when I knew I should have as I'd be by actually willing myself to kill those children.

❧

Too often, it takes destruction to end delusion. Although I had told my wife about Pam when I came home late that night, it took carnage the next day to look at Hannah as I do now, more precious than gold. But she still believes that no one cheats once, that after the line is crossed, the will to keep to one side is broken. Or perhaps she thinks the kind of person who would cross that line in the first place was always, and is always, the type to do it. Whatever she believes, I will spend the rest of my life trying to convince her she is wrong.

But that is only for her—whether I do hardly matters on my part, for I have been crippled by my weakness, knowing that no matter how things might have gone, ultimately it would have taken some tragedy to recognize the treasure I'd so selfishly abused.

We will never have children now. The cruelest thing she could have said, which I most deserve, was that she refused to have kids to a man who could not be true to his family. Above all, that hurts most.

And to think I believed I was in the business of saving lives. That can only happen, I know now, miles before we arrive.

So the chant laps against my mind, like the rhythmic swish of tires passing on the highway, *And* this *little piggy* . . .

MAINLAND

I was to meet Susan at the wharf restaurant. A vinyl shell there protected diners from the cool breezes and birds of the harbor, another Maine attempt at classic shorefront life, but one benumbed. And given the considerable tide fluctuations, most of the day, you could hardly call it a wharf, just a scaffold over the boulder and mussel-studded muck left in the cowering water's stead.

As I passed the bar, three men turned, the same ones I saw every afternoon I rode my bicycle back the neck of the peninsula from my fieldwork. They'd be leaning against the bed of a pickup backed up to the beach, as it was called—just the cobblestone edge of a cove—sipping beers and drawing on cigarettes, watching me. I met them one day.

The sheltered deck was busy with diners—empty-nesters and newlyweds, though not many of those—Castine is quite expensive. The exception was a family with a toddler, a little boy about to be a big brother.

I went to Susan, where she waved from a table next to the salt-stained and finger-smudged vinyl.

"I never thought to ask," she said as I pulled out my chair, "if you needed a ride."

I leaned my purse against the vinyl and sat. "The Hogans were happy to drive me. They tell me all the time to come to town for an evening."

"It can be hard," Susan said, passing me a drink menu, "staying somewhere alone."

"You've been there enough, doing your own fieldwork." I looked away, thinking of whether I wanted the house's amber ale or something exotic, not yet comfortable with this practical stranger. The three men at the bar watched us, heads leaned together, speaking. An unsettling image, the huddle before a play.

"I thought about what you said in Witherle Woods today," Susan said. "About how you reduce a thing by knowing it too well." She smoothed a crease in the tablecloth. "I have to admit that happens in my work."

The toddler drummed a spoon against the tray of his height chair. We both turned, and Susan chuckled. "Never again," she said, "will we see our worlds with a child's wonder."

She flushed, and my cheeks, too, warmed. We looked out at that inflating bay sparkling in the slanted sunlight.

There are points of clear demarcation in our lives, and her words marked one for me. They tentacled out and linked seemingly disparate incidents and impressions, which altogether have tinted the lens through which I've seen the world since. So much that happened just before and after that dinner gravitated and collided under the workings of larger forces, the way flotsam gathers into a cove by tow of moon and wind and current.

≈

The shape of the terrain remained, but little else had been left to its tendencies—bastardized woods, nothing virgin about them. A lot of human history here, I'd think every day as I ventured off the bike path, doing my inventory.

By classification Witherle Woods was forestland, so in my mind could not be littoral; I'd never seen anyplace along the east coast where woods forged so closely and solidly to sea, couldn't imagine that without the trees, I'd be within sight of a bay. Until an ocean breeze shouldered in, or a foghorn sounded in the harbor.

Witherle Woods was dense with spruce and fir, therefore aromatic of wintergreen, but in a dirty way, what with the must of its damp, needly humus. It was a bit medieval, I guess, with the mornings awash in mist and the gray-green pendants of lichen hanging from the evergreen boughs. Old man's beard, Mainers called it.

Just before I met Susan, nature had called. Thirty yards from the trail, I crouched to pee behind a glacial erratic boulder where I'd been on my knees combing among deadfalls for rare plants. I caught a flash through the trees, up-trail. A yellow windbreaker. A mountain biker. Damn.

I tugged my jeans under the shirttails of my denim shirt—no time to zipper—and ran toward my bike lying in the path where I'd thought, as always, I'd venture only a few steps away.

"Shit." This came from the rider, bicycle brakes moaning, and tires skidding on a patch of damp granite. Then the clatter of the chain slapping metal, the percussion of the bike frame against the ground, and the yellow jacket crashing in the debris of branches and leaves.

"I'm so sorry," I said, stretching my shirt downward.

The biker had known to roll as she landed on her shoulder. Already getting to her feet, she said, "Are you all right?"

"Me?"

She brushed spruce needles and dirt from the side of her bare leg and nodded at my bike in the path.

"Yes," I said. "It was nothing. You're not hurt?"

She thought a second, said no, and looked up and down the trail. "What are the odds? One crash breeding another. Out here."

"And I never see anybody on a weekday," I said.

Then she spotted the backpack I'd left by the boulder. She was older than I was, mid-thirties, in great shape with muscular thighs that broadened right into her sturdy hips.

"Are you from Castine?" she said, stepping to her bike where it lay behind mine. She pulled hers from the trail.

"No," I said. "Here for a month." I reached for my bike—stiffly, careful not to let my pants fall—and pushed it away.

"I'm Susan," she said.

"Robin," I said. We shook hands. "Are you from Castine?"

"Sheesh. I couldn't afford it. But unlike the ones who can, I do work here."

A breeze waggled the tops of the evergreens, the salty-fish air of the bay breaching the forest. It felt foreign and invasive, something I should jot in my inventory notes.

"I'm working here, too," I said. "Right here." I waved a hand around the woods, then grasped the bottom of my shirt where I felt coolness. I was sure my wide-open zipper had shown.

Susan's eyes had followed my wave but stopped again on my backpack. She knitted her brows.

"I'm an ecologist," I said. "Not a bootlegger or whatever you're thinking." I laughed. "I guess I should say I'm *becoming* an ecologist. It's a grad internship, inventorying this property."

"I do something similar." Susan unstrapped her helmet. "But in the ocean." She flicked her thumb seaward, a crescent of dimple edging each side of her mouth. She was easing, as people do when they discover a common root. But I immediately sensed a pecking order, patronage in the slight cant of her head. I liked that.

Susan took off her helmet and stepped to a hip-high rock where she sat and stretched her legs before her, rubbing her thighs. She combed her fingers through her hair, chestnut like mine, but longer, with sheaves of lighter streaks. "I'm a marine biologist at the Maritime Academy," she said. "I study lobsters." She nodded at our bikes. "So land and ocean have collided, in a way."

"Flora and fauna, too." I matched her grin at the vagary. "Plants of the land, animals of the sea."

"So why this particular place?" Susan said.

"It's a natural heritage program." I explained how the department of conservation cataloged rare plants across the state. "Witherle Woods is my tract."

Susan looked impressed. "I didn't think Castine was a hotbed for exceptional plants."

"It's not. I wish I expected some exciting find, but this was a personal destination, a place I wanted to see again." I glanced inland. "I could have picked somewhere pristine and away from the ocean, more suited to my background."

"Spent time here before, then?"

"Um-huh. At an inn—came for a getaway." Disappointment sneaked into my voice. Having already exhausted my nostalgia, I'd been left to mood-less, long days canvassing that knoll of third, maybe fourth-growth timber. I was more likely to find a cannonball than a rare plant; Castine had been home to forts and conflicts for hundreds of years, under four flags. The very trail I stood on was a former British artillery road.

I shrugged. "It was still a nice surprise to find so much of the peninsula forested. My first time here, I'd thought of Castine as mostly vacation homes."

Susan watched me, big-sisterly patience that invited me to tell more. But I would only say that something in the geography had reeled me back. "There's almost a sense to it, like an iconography. Even Castine on a map has the shape of a symbol, the way it mushrooms out from a skinny stem." I nodded toward the neck.

Susan followed my nod. I watched her process all I'd said. "Lobster work," she said, "has its barren stretches."

The silence in which we turned seaward was not uncomfortable, despite the salt air brushing my cheek, penetrating the must and mint of the woods. An undercurrent of camaraderie flowed between us, naturalist and biker that we both were. It came as well, I sensed, from mutual respect for contrast, she of the coast, a studier of things of the ocean, and I, a life-long inlander inventorying forests. The encounter felt symbiotic, like the two parts of old man's beard, so ghostly ever-present on that knobby peninsula. It's a fascinating partnership of algae and fungus, the combination of which resembles neither. The colorless fungus contributes water, the main source of minerals, the green algae photosynthesizes food. Reproducing by simply breaking off, the lichen becomes ubiquitous.

In my ease, I eventually went on with why I'd returned to Castine—how I'd wanted to hear something spoken to me again. The problem, I admitted, was that though I heard it, I couldn't tell what it said, sure as I was that what spoke were the unusual shapes and contours of the mid-Maine coast, pronounced so boldly in that bulbous peninsula.

"Ever had a place speak to you like that?" I said.

She shook her head no, and I read in Susan's frankness that she felt as relaxed as I did. None of that New England guard of the men at the beach—cordial but territorial, their eyes enameled by the isolation of long, cold seasons, a residue of the indignity and defensiveness of living in a place most outsiders only appreciated in comfortable weather.

"You don't talk like a Mainer," Susan said.

I grinned. "I'm from Pennsylvania. I go to grad school in Orono."

"From away." Susan shrugged it off. "I did grad work at U-of-Maine, too. But—" she smiled—"a while before you. Where do you stay?"

I lifted my chin toward the mainland. "Back the neck. I rent rooms above a garage."

"You're alone?" She looked at my ring finger. "Single?"

"Yes." I spontaneously looked at her hand. But she wore blue biking gloves.

It couldn't be helped, the asking of status, the pinning down and categorizing. It was necessary, after all, much as I helped science better define a rare species by cataloging patterns in the interdependence of organism and environment, further indi-vidualizing the thing, paradoxically, by its unity with something else. But couldn't any species, a lichen, for instance, be defined adequately by its unique parts?

"So," Susan said, "are you looking for anything particular?"

"Excuse me?"

She turned up the palms of her gloves and glanced around the woods. "Species."

My cheeks warmed again, and I pulled down on my shirt-front. "My best hope for adding to the inventory is moonwort fern." I nodded seaward. "But they'd be nearer the shore."

"I'm always looking for the exception, too," Susan said. "But instead of a species, it's behavior."

At that, I realized the cause of a profound undertow of sadness tugging my soul. Though scientists are keen on mechanisms, I don't know that we'll ever understand the workings of the mind where one thought bumps another, no matter how dissimilar, to trigger awareness of what's bothering a person. Comfortable in Susan's company, I let it out.

"The more I see into a place," I said, "the smaller it gets, the less sublime. I wonder if I'm doomed to forever ruining my experiences."

While Susan considered this, the source of my gloom became clearer. I thought of how I could no longer call up the feeling I had of Witherle Woods the first time I entered them, when I knew little of their history, natural and human. "There's bliss," I said, "in the ignorance." I glanced away, thought aloud. "Maybe it's innocence."

Susan plucked at one of her biking gloves. "Knowing anything takes the romance out of it."

"No, it's more than romance. We reduce the thing itself. Cheapen it." I was suddenly ashamed to look at Witherle Woods. "We think we can corral everything into understanding. It doesn't matter if it's an ecosystem or a lobster, somehow we strip its presence in the process of defining it."

"Hmm," Susan said, eyeing me. "I always believed the opposite. I think of myself as esteeming lobsters."

Though it never would have before, that seemed proud.

⌒

"Your drinks," our waiter said, arriving with a tray, "are on the three gentlemen at the bar."

He placed my pina colada on a napkin; Susan took her frosty mug before he could set it down.

"This hasn't happened in ten years," she said and raised her drink toward the bar. "Not since I was single." She sipped her beer, arched her brows, and clarified. "The last time."

"Divorced?" I said.

She nodded, then lifted her chin toward the bar. "They're local, those guys."

"I kind of know them," I said. "From when I ride my bike back the neck. They drink beer along the beach, and I stopped once." I chuckled. "The beach. There's no such thing in Maine. At least as I know it."

Susan leaned and put an elbow on her chair back, a clubby pose I'd noticed among established academics—full of self-assurance I longed for. But in the way she tipped her head and shook her hair away from her ears, I saw how lingering youth imbued that maturity. It made her all the more a handsome woman.

"That comes from a Pennsylvania girl," she said.

"I spent my college summers working at the Jersey shore, and for years before that, my mother and I vacationed in Delaware. I just thought all the east coast had a buffer—sand and spartina flats where land and sea ease into each other. Then I came to Maine and saw the ocean butting up to stone. It's like earth and water are frustrated here. They can't come to terms."

I looked out our plastic barrier. The masts of moored sailboats twitched in the foreground of an evergreen slope across the harbor, another of Maine's countless, hilly peninsulas groping like beggars' fingers into the wind-chafed blue.

The scene, the alcohol, amplified the voice that had called me there. Something about it brought to mind the irony of studying natural life in a place that had endured storm fronts of civilization for 400 years, the ground of forts and massacres, of ships' cannonballs hurled from waters that remained an irreconcilable antithesis to the granite-crusted shore.

Susan was smiling at the men at the bar. She caught me watching and indicated the water. "It's this way other places. Not every coast is like the mid-Atlantic. Think of volcanic islands forever freshening their crusts."

"I've seen that." I sipped my colada, glanced at the three men, all grins now. "A friend and I went to Maui once." My stomach tightened as I remembered finding the island overrun by non-native plants. I told Susan how disappointed I'd been that I couldn't picture what it was like before the whalers arrived. "I found only a few true Hawaiian plants. But," I said, lightening with the high point of my trip, "one was exceptional. It grew on the slopes of the crater. Silversword." I whispered the name, drawing out the s's as I pinched together the tips of my thumb and middle finger to make an oval shape. "The leaves are daggery and hoary. And just once in its lifetime, it sends up a bulb of purple blossoms. Six gorgeous feet of flowers shooting into the Maui sky." I closed my hand into a fist. "Then it dies. Fifteen years and one flowering, just to send off its seeds and perish."

"The salmon of the plant world," Susan said.

I looked to the harbor. "Still, there's something different about this coastline."

"Maybe what you like here is how it isn't overrun by foreign species."

No, I wanted to say, it was somewhere in the futile poking of land into sea. Instead, I grinned and looked around. "Except tourists."

"I wonder sometimes," Susan said, "whether there really is such a thing as an invasive species. Maybe it all depends on how you measure your universe. We might just be speeding up natural processes."

This from a naturalist? "When plant migration is 'natural,'" I said, "other species have time to develop defenses."

Susan shrugged, raised her glass to the men, and drank. She obviously wanted them to see her finish the beer, wanted more flattery in another round. Rebel scientist, I thought, adventurer. There was something as appealing in the daring as in the mature poise and self-confidence it edged.

With the sun setting over the mainland, a streak of yellow caught in the cups of harbor ripples. "I read once," I said, tracing the trail of light to the far shore, "that we go to make big decisions where land and water make big decisions." I looked at

Susan. "But what draws me here has to do with how land and water remain unresolved."

"Hell," Susan said, "even the people here are unresolved about the water. I know fish culturists who can't swim."

The waiter came to take our order, placing new drinks before us, compliments again of the men, though I hadn't finished half of mine yet.

"I can never make up my mind," I said, scanning the menu. I thought a second, bit my lip, and creased my eyes at Susan. "Would it bother you if I had lobster?"

"Not at all, so long as you're not offended by me ordering the vegetable strudel." She toasted the men at the bar and took a gulp.

I watched them return her grin. "One of them is a lobster-man," I said. "They told me even he can't swim."

⌒

Every afternoon they leaned against the bed of a pickup backed up to the cove, each man holding a can of beer. They'd raise them in a salute, yell out offers of a cold one to break the ride. I could feel them shifting their stares between my face and my pumping legs. One day, more out of thirst for companion-ship than for beer, I stopped.

The so-called beach was a rubble of stone and mussel shell, its color the mottled purple and jaundice of a bruise. As I rode onto it, lifting my behind from the bicycle seat to break the bumpiness of the cobblestone, one of the men nodded in each direction, indicating where the road sloped up and away from the sides of the cove. "I'd have to push up those hills," he said.

"Those aren't hills," I said.

I stood alongside the truck, squeezing the frame of my bike between my legs. The man who'd spoken shook my hand. He had Napoleon's jutting eyes and peregrine nose, even the pensive lips, which in pictures seem to foretell the doom. But as we introduced ourselves—"Roddy," he said—the features honeyed into the obliging smile of a politician.

I nodded a greeting to the other two, the shorter one coming around to me. The last man remained leaning against the truck. He merely moved his chin up—very slowly—and looked down his face, as a proud horse does when you first show him a handful of oats.

The shorter one, standing at my side now, asked where I was from. "Himalaya?"

"Pennsylvania," I said.

"Ah," Roddy said, leaning back, elbows on the bedrail, "the land of many deer."

"Too many deer," I said.

"No such thing," the man across the truck bed said. He pulled a cigarette to his mouth, sized me.

Every group I've encountered has been a variation of those men: The outgoing talker—Ambassador Roddy; the little grinning devil you can't help but like—this one sidling up to me and sprouting horns as he offered his sandpaper hand; and the quiet loner who watches from a porch of private darkness he shoulders like a shell.

"I'm Darren," the one shaking my hand said, so frank he could have gone on to tell me he knew my father. He had a charm that made me think I held all his attention, a friendly counterweight to the brooder by the truck bed. Darren's smiling, mossy green eyes clashed with the indigo cove. His face had every reason not to be good-looking—oblong with an up-jutting pate, bald to the middle of his skull where he was graying, though he couldn't have been more than 35. Despite this and a nose long and crooked, his looks flew in the face of the science that says we rate attractiveness by body symmetry, that in it we instinctively recognize able providers. I agree the eye is pleased somewhere before reasoning, but it's an individual intuition, as in the way a certain painting strikes a mood in me but not in another.

Darren hopped onto the truck's rear tire and reached into the bed for my beer. He returned to my side and snapped the tab. "Maybe there really can be too many deer," he said, handing me the can. "Tell us how, Robin."

I nodded where the knoll of Witherle Woods rose above the cove. "They nip away all the wildflowers and shrubs, all the diversity. The forest can't evolve on its own terms. Animals that depend on the understory disappear."

"See, Terry," Darren said, turning an appeasing smile to the man across the truck bed, a stone studying his cigarette, "there can be too many deer."

I swigged my beer. It was warm and brothy, a cheap brand. The fortification I'd seen salts put up in the presence of outsiders was built in degrees here. However attentive Darren was, his curiosity was still rooted in caution. And polite Roddy, inoculated by his wedding ring from suggesting a come-on, nevertheless seemed remote, looked away in this break of silence. At least Terry, the brooder, was forthright in his insularity.

"So, what do you do?" Roddy finally said.

"I'm an ecologist. Here studying plant communities." Only at this did Terry look into my eyes, narrowing his. Suspicion spread to the other two, and I quickly added that I worked just in places like Witherle Woods. "Publicly-open reserves." I could see it registering: conservationist bureaucrat. From away, at that. "What do you guys do?"

"I'm a contractor," Roddy said. "Darren works for me. And Terry—" he nodded across the truck bed—"is a lobsterman."

Terry was gazing at his beer, cigarette wedged between fingers. Beyond him, a constellation of striped lobster buoys—red, black, and white—lolled in the cove. And in the background, the spruce green knoll of Witherle Woods, its granite skirt impermeable as Terry's scowl.

The peninsula was pinched tight where we stood, "off neck" locals called that marshy lowland from which Castine bulbed spadelike into the bay. I wondered whether the ancient British canal, which sliced through the nape of that slender neck to connect facing coves, technically made Castine an island.

Across the cove from Witherle Woods, I'd seen a pillared mansion on its own knoll, a white-fenced horse pasture stretching to the water. A lovely home, but at complete odds with its setting, something blown ashore from where it might have stood at the end of an avenue of broad, deciduous trees commanding a plantation.

I forced a heavy gulp. The silence was awkward, and I could think of nothing to break it but the mansion. They followed my nod. "Quite a place around the cove there," I said. "I've ridden my bike to the gate. Whose is it?"

They shrugged.

"You're kidding. You've lived here all your lives?" I saw I embarrassed Darren. He put his hands in his pockets, lost the impish grin.

Roddy tried to explain. "We don't drive that way. None of us have family over there."

Terry banged the bedrail. "I did." He stared hard at Roddy, a look that said, you know damn well. Then he addressed me. "Ninety years ago, my family sold that land to people from Boston. Just so my great-grandfather and his brothers could make payments on lobster boats." He brushed his beard from his collar. "All the while, crooks from Connecticut smuggling shorts to where they're legal. Now you mind this." He pointed at me. "People come and go here all the time. People that got nothing to do with the place, that step no farther in it than them big houses and inns and golf courses." He grunted, guzzled beer. "Till it's too damn cold for their sweet asses."

"C'mon, Terry," Roddy said, "we'd never make it without the summer people."

Terry held an unlit cigarette toward Roddy. "You wouldn't." We all followed his glance out the cove, toward the mansion. "We never caught back up," Terry said. "My grandfather. My dad. We been hardly getting by since."

Darren crushed his can and threw it into the truck bed. Roddy handed him another and asked me if I was ready. I held up my can and sloshed the beer.

We'd had the beach to ourselves. Now a compact car, likely a vacation rental, parked along the road. A woman in shorts, her shirt unbuttoned over a bathing suit, got out and reached into the back to unstrap a child from a car seat. A man took beach toys out of the trunk.

"Finally," I said, "people here to actually swim."

Roddy and Darren grinned, and Terry snorted a laugh. The family walked not toward the beach but across the road to a rectangular pond enclosed by a cyclone fence. I'd seen a sluice from the bay feeding the pond at high tide through a pipe under the road.

"They're going to the pool," Roddy said.

"A swimming pool? Across from a beach?" I laughed and shook my head at the irony. "You spend your lives beside a bay, but don't go in." I thought of pools at oceanfront resorts in Maui, yards from beaches, how proud that seemed. But somehow, it struck me as the opposite here.

Terry indicated the cove by flicking ashes that way. "I'd like to see you swim in that cold water. And by the way, it's a river, no matter what everybody calls it. The Penobscot."

"It is?" Darren said.

Roddy, the referee, spoke up, voice eager to smooth this crumbling conversation. "The pool's hardly warmer. Just a mud-bottomed tide pond, really. A place for us to learn to swim."

My eyes traced the curve of cobblestone. The beach. "*Nobody* swims out there?"

"Depends on your definition of swim," Roddy said. "People wade."

Terry hacked out a smoker's phlegmy laugh. "Tourists. People from away."

His inhospitableness finally seeped to my nerves. It set them chattering against my effort to appear casual and comfortable. My breath stuttered, my beer can shook despite my wrist resting on my handlebar. The other two seemed to be spinning cocoons around themselves; Roddy sat on the tailgate now, swinging his legs while Darren stared at the ground, scratching his sideburns as if he pondered how that broad cove of tidal water could be a river. I breathed deep, summoned boldness, and poured out the beer—my announcement I was leaving.

Darren reached for the empty can and gave a soft grin of apology. To lift my spirits, he spoke with a caressing tone, the words channeled in a jab at Terry. "I know of lobstermen," he said, "can't even swim." He tipped his head toward the cove. "Never step foot in the water."

I smiled in thanks. But only for an instant—that impermeable bluff of a man at the truck seemed to distend over the beach, stealthily as the cold blue mega-tides of the gulf of Maine.

꩜

The constant tilt of Terry's eyes toward our table at the restaurant had the oppressive weight of his brooding at the beach. Even as he sipped beer or as Roddy or Darren said something in his ear, he watched. I accepted the third colada from them, but only because it might numb me to him. And I reasoned he was enamored with Susan. She was, after all, closer to his age.

Susan slid her hand to the middle of the table. "So tell me about this peculiar attraction to the Maine coast."

I concentrated on my drink's milky froth. "I guess it's because I always end up like that surf. I crash before I take to anything, never getting myself completely there." I looked at Susan. She'd canted her head, eyes slightly narrowed. "Even my grad program is feeling that way," I said. "I started out with visions of an unspoiled Maine forest, rare plants everywhere. Then came this bright idea."

Susan's close scientific scrutiny hemmed me into a corner of mirrors, my discontent echoing in reflections a thousand times over.

"I've been around fickle students a while now," she said. "Most just need to relax and give in to themselves. They typically answer a calling they'd spent all their energy pretending against."

She came across neither rude nor condescending, instead straightforward as if she stood before a tank of lobsters relating a social structure they'd perfected. She capped it off by lifting her glass, a gesture to both the men at the bar and me. She was so at ease—with the place, herself, her vocation. I envied that.

"So you're a native Mainer," I said.

"Salt in my blood."

I leaned into the table and teased. "Do you, a Mainer who studies lobsters, actually go into the ocean? Or are you a misogynist of the sea like these lobstermen I hear about?"

"Actually," she said, taking me very seriously, "I dive."

"And what do you see down there?"

"Sex." She shifted her shoulders over the back of her chair as the waiter placed her vegetable strudel on the table. "I study lobster sex."

The waiter set out my plate and a fresh drink for each of us. "These," he said, nodding toward the bar, "are compliments of the bearded one."

I followed his nod. Terry gave no expression, just a stare of acknowledgment to Susan's wave. It could as well have been a challenge.

"That's a male," Susan said. She pointed her butter knife at my lobster.

I slid my fork under the tail, lifted it, and peeked.

"You'll never find a penis there," Susan said, chuckling. "Genitals are not always obvious." She tapped a bulbous upper claw. "I know by how big these are." She leaned ahead and whispered. "But if you must know, lobsters actually have *two* penises."

I, too, leaned ahead. "Double trouble." And we burst out giggling.

Susan's eyes teared, and hard as she tried, she couldn't speak. She kept holding up her finger and sipping at her beer to extinguish the laughter, but every time erupted again, and it would catch with me. We guffawed all the harder when we noticed Terry watching, seemingly embarrassed, before looking away. Everybody in the restaurant cast eyes on us, even the little boy in the height chair.

Oblivious to the onlookers, Susan panted out, "There's no justice for a lobster, boy or girl." And though she paused and composed herself, her whisper was no less loud. "His penises are so tiny they couldn't penetrate even if the female had a vagina."

I intentionally met the eyes around us to make them look away. "No vagina?"

Susan shook her head. "He deposits sperm in a receptacle. The female carries it around for months until she's ready to extract her eggs." She scrunched her brows. "Such an ugly term—receptacle."

With a glance, I indicated the three at the bar. "Appropriate, though, from the male point of view." I frowned at my lobster. "So what's it like? Some sort of molestation?"

Susan stiffened with mock formality. "Robin, may I touch your lobster?"

I clasped my hands at my chest. "Well, I've never . . ."

Pushing aside her plate, Susan picked up my lobster and set it before her. "The act is quite tender." She took from her lap her napkin—cranberry-colored like the lobster—folded it lengthwise, and held it in the middle as she would another lobster.

"Before she could mate," Susan said, waving the napkin, "the female had to shed her shell. So she's very fragile." She aimed the napkin into the lobster's face. "To calm those big claws, she flushes scent through the water."

Most of the diners' eyes had gravitated back to us. The place went silent when Susan set down the napkin and began walking my lobster on-end. "He circles the female and strokes her." She tilted the lobster and brushed its antennae across the napkin.

Crude as the mime was, Susan puppeted with proficiency, her cropped-nailed, scientist's fingers nimble and tender in choreographing this moment of intimacy, the movements at once adroit, motherly, erotic. A man somehow could not carry out this scene.

"I've seen the foreplay go on for half an hour. Quite gentle and patient lovers, these brawny boys."

She moved the lobster to the end of the napkin. "Then the male approaches from behind and gently, ever so gently, uses his legs to turn her." Robin rotated the napkin and eased the lobster down. "Face to face, they begin fanning their every appendage, faster and faster."

As she stroked the napkin with my lobster, I forgot the Friday night patrons watching Susan's gentle love directing; I was enthralled with this hard-shelled animal doing soft porn on our tablecloth. The lovers may have been a dead shellfish and a napkin, but at the bottom of my spine, warm butter churned. I knew not whether it was from a perverse eroticism I found in the theatrics of inanimate objects or the virtuosity of the director's movements.

Susan held the thorax of the lobster with one hand, and with the other, began spanking its tail against the napkin. She looked at me. "They madly thrash against each other. Then he thrusts his hard little penises against her and spills semen into the receptacle." She grinned, bit her bottom lip, and looked down at the lobster. "Aah," she said, giving a final jab with the tail. "Then he dismounts. And get this—" she set down the lobster, the napkin's faintly tapered waist moist from the body of the seducer—"he eats her shell."

"Missionary," I said, staring at my lobster.

"Yep. And yet he never actually penetrates her."

"Never," I repeated.

Meeting eyes, we were too tipsy to contain those grins that want to squeeze out in the silence following awkward moments. My cheeks warmed, and I looked away. Faces turned like falling dominoes, some amused, most appalled. Roddy and Darren, at either side of Terry, were all smiles. They pretended to wipe sweat from their brows, gave silent claps, and swiveled back to the bar.

But Terry neither smiled nor turned away. He studied me, his stare so intense his face inched forward. That warm butter at my loins congealed, and I held up my plate for Susan to return my lobster.

≈

I squeezed the juice of a lemon wedge onto my final forkful of claw meat and plucked it off with my teeth. I chewed slowly, luxuriating my tongue in the perfect al dente of that briny flesh. I swallowed it with the last of my colada, pleasantly dizzy now from the softer buzz of alcohol that comes on a full stomach.

"Here comes one of our princes," Susan said.

Darren approached, smiling at Susan, hand out. He merely nodded at me, and I wondered whether the jab of jealousy I felt came from being slighted by my protector at the beach or if I resented losing Susan's attention. And she certainly lavished it on Darren.

"You fellows are quite generous," Susan said, taking her hand from his, lifting her empty glass. "Pull up a seat."

"I was just about to ask if you'd join us at the bar," Darren said.

I shook my head. "I'd rather stay here."

"Join *us* then," Susan said and waved for the others.

$\backsim$

The cove skulked low and steely under heavens clear of all but a quarter moon. I pulled Susan's car off the road as Roddy backed his pickup to the beach's high tide line. When I suspected this meant he planned to be there until the water rose after daylight, my heart plunged so fast my fingers numbed.

I'd rather have been anywhere else, but I would not abandon Susan. Watching her down three more beers at the restaurant, I'd decided she had either a drinking problem or a problem that needed drinking. The situation at our table had developed into attempts at pairings, as such scenarios always do by default or attrition or—on the rare occasion—choice. By last call, Darren had his arm around the back of Susan's seat and had suggested we go to the beach for a private party. Roddy, with his wedding ring, had obediently distanced himself at a chair he'd turned from the next table, which left Terry seated at my side. He commanded my periphery, the constant sentinel-presence of a lighthouse, but heavy and unsafe with a feeling that he interpreted entitlement in the circumstances. Every time some witticism from Darren compelled me to politely smile, I knew I was sending encouragement.

The men stumbled out of the pickup, Roddy keeping the driver's door open so that light shined into the bed. Beside me, Susan fumbled with the handle, stepped out, and steadied herself against the car as she started away.

I tightened my stomach muscles, opened the car door, and followed two steps behind like a wary dog.

At the tailgate, Susan hopped up between Roddy and Darren, the frizzes of her hair illuminated like a diadem in the truck's cab light. Darren handed her a beer and offered me one. "No thanks," I said and leaned against the truck bed. I looked out at a stain of light at the edge of the cove on the mainland side. From the mansion, I guessed.

Across the truck bed, Terry lit a cigarette and unrolled his sleeves, his shirt a crisper blue and white version of the flannels he wore the other days I saw him here.

I was gathering resolve to tell Robin I needed to go home, that I had to work the next morning, when Roddy held up his watch to catch the cab light. "My wife's gonna kill me," he said. He leaned back, looking behind Susan at Darren. "I don't want to break up the party."

The three of them looked over their shoulders at Terry and me, brows raised like eager kids. "Anyone mind," Roddy said, "if I leave you here with Susan's car?" I caught Darren putting his hand on Susan's knee.

If I'd asked, I'm sure Roddy would have taken me to the Hogans. But something trumped even the foreboding from that man across the truck bed. I wish I could say my reason for staying was to watch over Susan, but it was more in hopes of recovering my notion of her. I stepped away from the truck as Roddy came round the driver's side and thanked me. Then he left the four of us standing in the dark.

◈

"I need to go pee," Susan said.

I stepped toward her, relieved. But she slipped her hand into Darren's and asked if he'd ever seen Elephant Rock.

He looked at the water. "Tide's low—we can make it."

I reached for Susan's other hand. She pulled it back, winced. Moonlight shone enough for me to see her face un-tauten, sharp annoyance giving to confused embarrassment. She tilted her head, studying me as best she could. Then the embarrassment was mine; she made a tsk that said *poor girl*.

"You have the car keys," she said, stepping back, "if you and Terry want to wait there." And I let her slip away, the chomping of cobblestone fading toward the mainland, toward the fleeing glow of Roddy's headlights.

I pulled my jacket tight and looked out at the cove. At the edge of my vision, the glow of Terry's cigarette arced to and from his mouth. Finally, the chill turned me toward the car. I did not speak, fearing that whatever I said might sound like an invitation. He followed anyway.

Getting in, he reached into his shirt pocket and asked if I minded him smoking.

"Of course I mind."

He snapped open a beer he'd taken from the truck, sipped, held it out to me. I looked away.

He said, "Gotta man?"

I closed my eyes, put the keys in the ignition, and asked him to *please* get out.

"Girl, maybe?"

"Get *out*."

"We might as well get along," he said, setting his beer on the dash. "We're gonna be here for a while." And the instant I reached for the horn, he had hold of my wrist.

"Do not touch that," he said.

Between the deliberate spacing of his words was the clear threat of a broken arm. And yet, though panic wrung my throat of word and breath, the moment felt a matter of course, so consistent was it with the nature of that place. My trained eye, keen to patterns in landscapes, had read message after message of conflict—encrusted peninsulas jutting into bays; the pummeling surf; men of the ocean who could not reconcile themselves with the ocean; salty air, un-brackish against the menthol of spruce. As despairing as was the sense of inevitableness, I found in it strength, a resolve that did not cede, a holding of ground.

"Don't fight," Terry said, almost soothingly. "It'll be better. For both of us." He loosened his grip but drew me closer—to the point my shoulders twisted awkwardly between the seatbacks. He put his other hand to my chin, pushed it back, then unzipped my jacket. "Thatta girl," he said and coursed his knuckles down my chest to my stomach. When he squeezed his fingers between my thighs, he let out a moan, wheezily smothered in the ferment of cigarettes and beer.

But I stared out at that light on the cove and squeezed my knees tight, anchoring my quaking nerves.

He twisted my wrist, moved the other hand to my throat. "I told you, don't fight it."

"Why not?" I said. "Isn't that how it should be?"

The words quickened his breath. He tilted my chin again. Still, I held my eyes straight-ahead, sat firm and impervious as granite. When he moved his hand back down my chest, untucked my shirt, and palmed my stomach, scales shed away, some outer layer of me brittling to detritus. He reached for my bra, flake after flake falling, and I willed myself deeper to stone.

No woman is an island unto herself, I heard my mother say times she found me sulking away my adolescence as I huddled on the porch swing or lay curled on my bed. And I'd look for an isthmus, for an ebb in the tides that isolated me. But I never found so much as a reef. Why, I always wondered, why did those tides overrun all my human connections?

By then, he'd tugged up my bra, the elastic squeezing tight at my armpits. He was stroking my breasts, paring away the layers. And I continued to watch that light hold against current and tide. He would not reach within.

He must have sensed this. He let go of my wrist, and instead of touching me elsewhere, reached for himself. Frittered to the core, I held still effortlessly, the soul of stone at which sculptors must surrender.

I recall the mounting lap of his respiration, the hot reek of his habits and lust. Then he fixed himself and leaned his head against the window. He fell asleep.

I remained unmoving until that spot upon the swelling water gave to the jaundiced light of dawn, and Susan and Darren returned. At the car window, Susan was apologetic, Darren pleading excuses like a teenager arriving home late. I ignored them and opened the door.

My jacket and shirt were off before I crossed the debris of kelp and shell strung along that cobblestone demarcation. I stepped on my heels to remove my shoes and waded into the cove, stopping only to bend and take off my jeans. The water up to my panties, my bra still twisted above my breasts, I fell forward into the cold, saline waters of the gulf.

I swam. I skimmed buoyantly across the depths, numbing to the ache in my arms and legs, abandoning, I understood, my search for attachment. Then I treaded water, looking back where the pair stood insignificant against the landscape. I awoke to its pure beauty. These were not peninsulas reaching to conquer the sea. Each abided, anticipating an eternal promise, even as that promise remained un-apprehended beneath the great and mysterious design.

Virginal, articulate, eloquent, that beauty bespoke how restraint esteems fecundity. Bliss in abstinence is the worship of fertility. I released myself to such firmness, handed to faith my needs of the moment, and awaited in my benumbed and bathed flesh the promise.

My lips shivered as the cold reached my pith. I swam farther, freed in knowing that in my humanity, I did not have to abide by nature. And there was both empowerment and humility of spirit. A woman may be an island unto herself. Worthily.

I turned back.

&

So now I find the Maine coast lovely, jutting and impermeable as it is. Lobstermen who cannot swim, after all, are no less hunters. I find, too, people who abide as islands no less beautiful. No less than those who follow their isthmuses to the safely mapped mainland.

THE END

ABOUT THE AUTHOR

Photo by David A. Woodring

PJ Piccirillo is the author of *Heartwood* and *The Indigo Scarf*, a Sunbury Press SUNNY Award winner. He has twice won the Appalachian Writers Association Award for Short Fiction. An advocate of northern Appalachia's under-recognized literature, PJ is the founder of the Writers Conference of Northern Appalachia (WCoNA) and the *Northern Appalachia Review*, for which he is the current editor-in-chief.

Inspired by the timberlands and red brick industrial burgs of Pennsylvania's Allegheny Plateau where his ancestors settled to work woods, farms, tanneries, mines and rail sections, Piccirillo's stories are as recognized for their sensitivity to their characters' passions as for their depictions of conflicted hearts taking on their demons.

PJ is a third-generation community firefighter, an EMT, NASCAR firefighter, winemaker, and Cubmaster. He's been a factory worker, campground owner, marketing manager, technical writer, and cook. He can be found with his wife and three sons pursuing all things outdoors on the creek-fissured plateau of his native northcentral Pennsylvania.

Made in United States
North Haven, CT
18 June 2024

53779571R00104